GONE AGAIN

KATRINA MARIE

For all my people pleasers out there. Don't let others steal your joy. Be unapologetically you!

Chapter One

Audrey

I COULD BE DOING SO many other things tonight. For instance, I could catch up on *Project Runway*. Or, I might even get caught up on my laundry. Hell, I could be washing my hair. But no. Instead, I'm sitting in a restaurant with these lovey-dovey couples planning Stella's wedding.

Don't get me wrong, I'm happy for my cousin. She finally let go of her weird obsession with work and started enjoying the little things in life. She's happier than she's ever been. I only wish it could have been us girls only.

Of course, wherever Tiffany goes, Spencer follows. That wild child found someone that keeps her leveled out. I never thought I'd see that day come. He's good for her, though.

While it fills me with joy to see my cousins so ridiculously in love, it makes me feel like the third wheel. I've been avoiding both of them for months. It's just hard seeing them glow because of their relationships when I can't seem to find anyone who completes me. Gah, could I sound any more like a sappy love movie? I haven't been truly happy since the day Justin dumped me our senior year of high school. I've gone on dates just to see if there is some sort of spark with anyone else, but they are all dull in comparison to him.

It's stupid to never move on, I know that. But I moved to this city in the hopes that maybe I'd run into him. Maybe with us being older and away from his dad, we could give things another go. My cousins thought it was because I wanted to be closer to them, and that's partly true. It's not the whole truth, though. I knew Justin was going to Hilltown University. I was supposed to go with him. We had our whole future planned out. It hurt too much then to go to the same college. I couldn't be in the same vicinity of the boy who destroyed my faith in relationships.

I hoped it would give me the space I needed to heal. To get over my high school sweetheart. It didn't. When Stella asked me if I wanted to be her roommate until we both got our feet beneath us, I jumped at the chance. I needed to get out of my town and all the memories I shared with Justin. The only way to do that was to start over completely.

Tiffany nudges me in the ribs with her elbow.

"What the hell is that for?" I whisper loud enough only for her to hear.

"Stella is talking about dresses. Get out of your head and pay attention."

Geez. When did she become so serious? I know this is important for both Johnny and Stella. I just don't understand why the planning has to be such a big production. Yes, it's important, but this could have been done at one of our apartments. Or, with just us girls. I'm really hoping there's more of that in the future. Not that I don't love Johnny and Spencer, but they are distracting from things that need to be done. And maybe I'm being a baby because I don't have anyone to cozy up to. This is all just too much.

It's a reminder of what could have been. What would have been if someone's parent wouldn't have gotten in the way. It pisses me off that his dad got married not long after Justin went off to college. He seemed lighter when I saw him around town. Where was all that understanding when his son was dating me? Why was I not good enough for his son to be with? Nope, my mind can't go there. Not tonight. I won't let.

"What do you think about burnt orange for your dresses?" Stella asks.

I haven't been listening, but that color definitely caught my attention. "Please don't make us be a college cliche," I whine. "If it's what you really want, I'll wear it, though." The color would look awful with Tiffany's hair. It makes sense that she would choose it since she wants a fall wedding. I hope she looks at other colors.

"I'll go ahead and mark it out. Y'all don't seem too excited about it," she sighs. "If you wouldn't have said anything, Tiff's face did."

The cousin in question bursts into laughter. "Who would have thought it'd be sweet Audrey that would object to that horrific color. She usually goes along with whatever." She's not wrong. I'm very go with the flow…to an extent. I don't like surprises, and tend to stick to myself. Okay so I'm nothing like Tiffany. Maybe that's what's wrong with me.

Nope. Not going down that road again. It's not a good headspace to be in. Why the hell does Justin keep popping into my thoughts? Is it because Stella is getting what I should have already had? My fairytale, happily ever after. I need to get out of this mood. If I don't, I won't be any help to her or anyone else.

Even though I'm alone and not completely happy, I can't help but feel excited for Stella. This is something I never thought I'd see with her. At least, not for a very long time. Men weren't even on her radar until she met Johnny. But I need a break from the stolen kisses and planning. "I'll be right back."

I walk toward the back of the restaurant so they know I'm not leaving. The restroom is the closest escape I can think of. The chatter from the patrons is barely audible as I close the restroom door. Finally, peace and quiet. I know Tiffany means well, but she didn't have to call me out like that in front of Stella. I refuse to be the third wheel. The realization that most people take dates to weddings finally dawns on me. Crap, I'm going to have to find a date. Maybe I can ask someone in accounting to come as my plus one. It's not ideal but I don't see myself finding my soulmate between now and Stella's wedding.

My reflection in the mirror is pale, and I look exhausted. I've basically turned into Stella. Well, the Stella that existed before she went to Asheville. I've thrown myself into work and doing things around my apartment. Anything to keep me occupied and not have to go out with Tiffany and Spencer.

Minutes pass by and I'm still not ready to go back out there. If I don't, someone will come barging in looking for me. Tiffany and Stella have zero patience, especially if they think I'm acting weird. I step back through the door. My gaze on my feet as I walk through the restaurant to the table.

Someone blocks my path and I slam into them. Liquid

splashes all over me, the person, and the floor. Shit, and now I've knocked someone's drink out of their hand. "I'm so sorry," I say before I look up. My eyes meet warm brown eyes I could never forget, and I gasp. No way. There's no way in hell I would run into him...here. But here he is. The guy who broke my heart all those years ago and who I still see in my dreams to this day. It's as if my thoughts conjured him.

"Audrey?" My name spills from his lips and all I can think about is the way we used to lie on the hood of his car and stare at the stars. Talking about our futures.

I can't do this. Not tonight. Not ever. I thought he moved to Dallas for fuck's sake. He's not supposed to be here anymore. I don't bother going back to the table. I'm running through the restaurant and out the front door. Stella and Tiffany calling my name before the door cuts off their voices.

Chapter Two

Justin

THERE'S ABSOLUTELY nothing that could have prepared me for that. To run into the girl, no woman, I loved all those years ago. My shirt is drenched, the sticky alcohol seeping through, and my mouth wide open as the only person I've ever truly cared about flees from the restaurant.

I didn't know she lived in this area and I've done my share of social media stalking under the guise of making sure she ended up happy. She must have everything on tight lockdown or I might have sought her out. I've lived here since I graduated from college and haven't run into her once. Austin is big, but it's not *that* big.

"Excuse me." A guy wearing an apron steps in front of me. "Is there any way you can move over? I need to get this cleaned up before someone falls and hurts themselves."

How long has he been trying to get my attention? It doesn't matter because my feet start in the direction of the door Audrey just flew out of. I need to make sure she's okay. "Sorry, man."

He waves me off. "It's not the first time and it won't be the last."

I'm almost to the hostess stand. The lights from outside fill the window next to the door. I'm so close, but a hand grabs my arm and I stop in my tracks. "What the hell are you doing here?"

A redhead in her twenties is glaring at me. Hatred coming through loud and clear. I have no clue who this woman is, but something wiggles in the back of my brain telling me I'm wrong. "I'm not sure what you mean." Glancing around the restaurant, I pull my arm from her grasp. "Last time I checked, I'm free to dine wherever I wish."

"Maybe," she shrugs her shoulders. "What did you say to her?"

"Say to who?" I'm honestly confused. I haven't said anything to anyone…except for Audrey before she ran out.

A tall blonde, who I do recognize rushes toward us. "Tiffany," she spits. "Stop being rude."

No way. This can't be happening. I know exactly who this is. She's not so little anymore, and it seems like her temper has gotten worse over the years rather than better. "Holy shit. You grew up," I laugh, not able to hold it in. I should have known it was her when Stella walked up. That's one thing I remember from my time dating Audrey. When Stella was in town, all three of them went everywhere together. I see not much has changed since then.

"Seriously, that's what you have to say to me?" She raises a finger and pokes me in the chest. "You. Broke. My. Cousin's. Heart." Each word is driven home with a jab.

Stella looks confused. "What do you mean? Audrey told me it was mutual."

Tiffany gives her cousin a pointed look. "That's because she was too sad and didn't want you to worry." She shifts her gaze to me again. "I'm going to go look for her. You," she points her finger at me again, "Stay away from her."

I don't really have a choice in that matter since I couldn't get ahold of her if I wanted to. Audrey became a ghost when I left for college. I wanted to see her when I went home to see my family, but she wasn't there. My dumb ass assumed she'd gotten over us and was off living her own adventures. Apparently breaking up with her messed her up pretty bad. It's not something I'm proud of. Hell, I didn't even want to do it. But I didn't have much of a choice. Things my dad said made sense...in a weird twisted way.

Tiffany runs out of the restaurant. A tall guy with glasses walks over and shakes his head. "I'll go after them, Stella." He leans in and hugs her. I'm not sure who this guy is. Is he here with Tiffany, or Audrey? I hope like hell it's the former. They are standing pretty close to me and I hear him whisper, "Congrats on the engagement. Don't worry about the bill. I paid it when I saw Tiffany stomp over here." He steps back. "With the fury in her eyes, I kind of figured the night was over."

"Thanks, Spencer." Stella gives him a small wave. "Text me when you find them and I'll come over."

"Will do," he salutes. "Johnny should be over here in a bit." He looks over at me, but I can't decipher what it means. It's like understanding hits him, and before I can question it, he leaves.

Stella faces me once again. "Want to fill me in on what

just happened? One minute Audrey is fine and the next she goes to the restroom before running out of the restaurant like the hounds of hell are on her feet. What did you do to her?"

Why do they all think I did something to her? I was minding my own business, walking back to the bar when she ran into me. How am I the one to blame? "I didn't do anything. She ran into me when she came out of the restroom, I guess. The only thing I said was her name and she took off."

"So, you didn't say anything else to her?" She crosses her arm and taps her foot. Geez. This is one thing I did not miss about the three of them being together. When one of them gets pissed off, all of them have to throw in their two cents. You'd think they'd get tired of fighting each other's battles.

"No," I deadpan. "I didn't say anything. She didn't give me a chance."

"Did you know she was here?"

I guess the interrogation isn't over yet. "No. I haven't seen her since I left town. I didn't even know she was living here until about five minutes ago when she ran into me...literally."

"So, what happened way back then? Clearly, that is what caused her reaction."

A man comes up behind her, I'm assuming Johnny, and wraps his arm around her. "Stop questioning him," he rolls his eyes. "That's kind of private."

"There are no secrets between me and my cousins." But the fact that she doesn't know what really went down is proof that there are.

I can't deal with this right now. Not when Audrey is somewhere out there, so distraught she couldn't even handle me saying her name. "Look, you'll have to ask her. In the meantime," I pull my wallet out of my back pocket and grab a business card. "Can you call me when you find her so I know she's okay."

"Why do you care? You didn't bother trying to see her after things went south with y'all." She crosses her arms over her chest, waiting for my reply. What does she want me to say? I haven't seen any of them in close to ten years.

I open my mouth, even though I have no idea how I'm going to answer, but Johnny intervenes. "Drop it, Stella." He reaches for my hand holding the business card and pulls it from my fingers. "Audrey is a big girl and can handle herself. Just because you're the oldest doesn't mean you need to come charging over here like a mama bear protecting her cub." He gently pushes her toward the exit, and nods at me, "I'll give you a call when I know what's going on."

"No, he won't," Stella grumbles under her breath, but I hear her anyway. They don't say anything else to me and leave.

I'm still trying to process what exactly happened tonight. And what was Tiffany going on about? Audrey acted fine when we went back to school. I mean we avoided each other, sure. But she didn't seem to upset about our break up after the first couple of weeks.

Nobody knows, but she's the one I let go of when I shouldn't have. Despite what I wanted, I listened to the one person that was supposed to have my best interests at heart. Seeing her tonight brings back all those memories from when we were younger, and I'm kicking myself for not trying harder to find her.

There's nothing I can do tonight, though. I have no way to contact her and I have no guarantee that Stella's fiancé will actually call me. I can only hope that he's a man of his word. I turn back toward the bar area, pay my tab, and tell the bartender to give the waiter who cleaned up my mess part of the tip. Someone should have a good night, at least.

Me? I'll be heading to my house…alone. It's not that unusual, but after seeing Audrey, I can't help wishing I had someone to go home to. I'm still not sure if that first guy is her boyfriend, but I'm hoping like hell he isn't. I wouldn't mind getting to know the woman she has turned into.

Chapter Three

Audrey

I. CAN'T. Breathe. It's not only because I bumped into Justin, though he's a big part of the reason. But, holy crap, I haven't ran in way too long. Why do people enjoy this? It's pure torture. My legs are on fire, and I'm going to go ahead and say this is my work-out for the week.

"Dammit, Audrey," Tiffany gasps from behind me. "Would you slow down? It's almost impossible to run in these heels."

I slow my pace until I come to a stop and look over my shoulder. Tiffany is doing this weird wobble run, and to people looking in, she probably appears drunk. Well, she is a little tipsy. She started drinking before we even made it to the restaurant. She justified it by saying she was "pre-gaming." Spencer settled her down, but not so much that she doesn't still imbibe more than she should during cele-brations.

She's within feet of me, and I take a deep breath. "It's about," I gasp trying to get the words out, "time you."

Another gasp. Seriously, I need to up my cardio. I know I've only gone a few blocks, but I shouldn't be this out of breath. It's ridiculous. "Caught up," I finally finish the sentence.

Tiff smacks my arm and rolls her eyes. "I would have a long time ago if I was in regular shoes." She taps her heel against the concrete and it's annoying. "Besides, I had to stop and tell off a certain someone."

I groan. "What did you say?"

A car speeds by and we both take an involuntary step back. The speed limit isn't very fast downtown, but if the roads are empty…not many people follow it. I'm not okay with either of us being roadkill because some jackass isn't paying attention and winds up on the sidewalk. Tiffany shrugs her shoulders, "That he better not talk to you."

"And that was it?" I really hope Stella didn't hear any of it. She doesn't know the extent of what our breakup did to me. She was away at college and I didn't want to bother her with my stupid high school drama. My cousin looks down at the ground, and that's all the answer I need to know that she said way more than she should have.

"I, um," she begins before she clears her throat. "I may have told him just how much he hurt you when he dumped you. And Stella may have told me that I needed to stop being rude."

"Ugh." Freaking Tiffany and her big mouth. "Why did you have to say anything? I was handling it."

The bubble of laughter that comes out of her mouth takes me by surprise. "You call running five blocks away from the restaurant handling it? I think we have different definitions of those words." I have no comeback prepared. She has left me speechless. "Be honest with yourself, cuz. You were running away like a scared little girl."

"No, I wasn't. I avoided a situation that could have gotten out of hand." Who am I lying to? If there's anyone who knows me better than I know myself, it's Tiffany. That's only because we grew up in the same town, right down the road from each other.

"You totally ran," a deep voice says from the darkness and I jump, almost falling backward. How in the world is he so freaking sneaky?

"You know it's not very nice to scare the hell out of people, right?"

Spencer wraps his arms around Tiffany from behind and leans his chin over her shoulder. Gah, seeing them being all couple-like makes me want to puke. Especially after the shit show back at the restaurant. "I wasn't exactly quiet. How is it my fault you weren't paying attention?"

"Whatever," I roll my eyes. "I'm going to assume the other two are right behind you."

"Maybe not right behind me," he bats away a strand of Tiffany's hair that gets in his face. "But it's a good bet that they'll find us soon enough."

"Stella is going to be pissed," I say to nobody in particular. "I can't believe I managed to ruin the night. That's totally your job, Tiff."

"There's no need to be an asshole," Tiffany huffs while leaning further into Spencer. "It's not my fault you don't know how to deal with guys."

She's wrong. I know how to deal with men. Just not this man. "I think I'm going to go home now."

Stella comes into view. "You're crazy if you think we're going to let you go home to mope by yourself. We are coming with you."

Tiffany turns toward Stella, "We are?" One chastising look from our oldest cousin and she knows it was the wrong thing to say. "I mean, yep, we are. I just need to run by our apartment first."

"For what?" Spencer looks dumbfounded, but he ought to know how this works by now.

"Alcohol, of course." She grins up at him, and I swear I just threw up a little in my mouth. "Little Miss Goody Two-Shoes over here," she hikes her thumb in my direction. "Never keeps a steady amount of booze at her place."

"Not all of us need a drink to have fun."

"Maybe not, but you need one to get over the shit storm that took place tonight. And you're going to drink until I think you'll have a hangover in the morning."

I shrug my shoulders. She has a point. I don't know if she has enough alcohol to wipe the night from my memory, but we can sure as hell try. "Are we ready to go to my place, then? As much as I like this city, I'm not a huge fan of having serious discussions on the side of the road."

"I'll go grab my truck and bring it around," Johnny announces before kissing Stella on the cheek and jogging off.

She definitely found the perfect guy. And I can't believe she's getting her happily ever after. The way Johnny looks at her makes me long for a relationship like that. One where you know you're the most important person to them. I used to have that…once upon a time. Then he dumped me without rhyme or reason. A few weeks later Justin was with someone else and I realized he didn't care about me as much as I did him. A tear escapes my eye and slides down my cheek. The old hurt coming back with a vengeance. Why did I have to bump into him tonight of all nights? It just had to be the one night that my cousins were here to witness it all. At least she'll have a funny or sad story to tell her future kids.

Stella comes closer to me and pulls me into her arms. "You obviously need to fill me in on a few details."

"Yeah, probably." I twist out of her hold, not wanting to feel like a child that can't handle heartache. "But it might not be tonight."

"That's fine. I'm here for you whenever you're ready."

"Do y'all want us to hang out here until Johnny pulls around?" Tiffany asks, bouncing on her toes. "If not, we're going to run by the apartment to grab the alcohol and meet you at your place."

"Go ahead," I nod toward the street. "We'll be fine." A kid whizzes past us on a skateboard. "It looks like we'll have a bunch of teens to keep up safe."

"Are you sure?"

"Yep. It won't take him long to get over here."

Tiffany is already walking backward, the way they came. She waves and smiles. "Love you and I'll see y'all in a few."

Not long after they've left, Johnny pulls up. Rather than sit in the front seat with her fiancé, Stella climbs in the backseat with me. I'm not sure why. It's not like I can do anything stupid with her in the same truck. Not that I would. Honestly, I think I'm still in shock. After all these years I never expected to run into him away from home. Hell, I didn't realize he was still in this area. I figured he moved off to whatever big shot job he was following.

Now, I need to figure out how to adjust to knowing he's in the same city as me. To know that I could potentially run into him again. I can't let those thoughts take root, though. He may be here, but it took years for me to run into him. What are the chances I'll run into him again?

Chapter Four

Justin

Walking into a dark, empty house has never bothered me before. Tonight, though, I want something more. Bumping into Audrey is completely throwing me off my game. She's making me question everything and not one single word passed between us. Well, except when I uttered her name. A part of me wonders if the guy Stella was with will actually call me once they find her.

I flip on every light switch I pass by on the way to my room. I've got to get out of these clothes. They are dry now, but I can feel the sticky residue from the whiskey. I still can't believe I ran into her. In this city of all places. Tonight was supposed to be low-key. A way to unwind after the meetings I've been in all day. The firm I work for is merging with another one. Normally I wouldn't have to attend any of the meetings, but with a promotion they came with the territory. My only hope is the transition will go smoothly. That's not likely to happen if I can't get Audrey out of my head.

I didn't even get a chance to eat anything. I peel off my shirt and pants, throwing them into the hamper. My stomach growls at the thought of food. I was going to take a quick shower but that will have to wait. Opening my dresser drawer, I pull out a pair of sweats and shove my legs into them. I'm not a hundred percent sure I even have groceries. Hopefully, there's something I can throw together, or at least have some cereal.

I walk out of my bedroom, but stop in my tracks. My phone is still in the pants I just took off. I need that in case that guy calls me. Hurrying back to the room, I pull the pants out of the hamper and grab my phone out of the pocket. The likelihood that he'll call is slim. I won't let that kill my hope, though. Sleep isn't going to come easily tonight if I don't hear that Audrey is home and safe. With my phone in hand, I can finally look for food.

I set down my phone before I pull open the pantry door and grab the first box of cereal I can find. It's not my favorite, but it will do. My stomach grumbles as I get a bowl and pour the cereal into it. Note to self…don't go almost all day without eating. It was entirely my fault, but that doesn't matter. I could have easily called for something to be delivered. The day just got away from me and when it was time to leave, I still hadn't eaten anything.

The air from the refrigerator is cool as I open it. It's almost bare, and I need to get some groceries. Taking my lunch will be imperative if this merger will be taking up most of my day. I doubt I'll have any downtime when we're moved into the new offices. My eyes land on the milk, and I open it, about to pour it into my cereal when a pungent smell hits me.

"Son of a bitch," I yell. Holding the jug of milk up to my

face, there are small chunks formed in what should be liquid. I can't believe I almost poured that in my bowl. I gag as I look at the date. This shit went bad almost two weeks ago. Looks like I'll be eating my cereal dry. It's just another punch to the gut on this shitty day. Setting the milk back in the fridge to deal with another day, I close the door and grab my bowl. It's not as satisfying, but it's better than nothing.

My phone vibrates against the countertop and I almost drop the bowl in my rush to answer it. I don't bother seeing who it is before I swipe it open to answer the call. "Hello."

"Why do you sound like you've been running?" Ugh, it's just my step-sister, Corrine. Dad finally found someone to put up with his grumpy ass and she came with a daughter that was older than me.

"Don't worry about it," I snap. I swear she drives me nuts. She may be older than me, but she acts like a little sibling way more than I do.

"Gah, who pissed in your cereal?" She just had to say that. I don't even want my cereal now. I'll call for delivery as soon as I get her off the phone.

"Nobody." It's a lie. She doesn't need to know that, though. "It's just been a weird day."

"Is this my chance to make it weirder?"

"I'm sensing there's a reason you're calling so late at night." Please don't let it be another call asking for money. It wouldn't be so bad, except that I just helped her with the down payment on her studio a few months ago. I have no problem helping her with her business ventures as long as she's turning a profit, and she has been. I would know. It was the one condition I had to helping her. I am the one that goes over her books. Who would have thought the small town we live in would be the bulk of her photography clients?

"Actually," she drawls, trying her best to build suspense behind whatever she wants. "How would you feel about me staying with you for a week or two?"

The laugh bursts from my lips before I have a chance to rein it in. "You can't be serious. Aren't we a little old for sleepovers?"

Corinne clears her throat, "Under normal circumstances, yes I would say we are. But this is for a good reason."

"And what's that?" I reach my hand up to rub my temples and realize I'm still holding the bowl of cereal. I set it down and wait for her answer.

"Do you remember that guy I was dating?"

"How could I forget? He was kind of a dick."

"That's the problem. We broke up and he can't move out of my house for another week or so."

"He is living with you?" It shouldn't surprise me, but it does. I thought she was smarter than that. I can't even count how many times I've told her not to jump into being serious with someone, and she does this.

"Look," she huffs. "I know I'm a dumbass for letting him move in with me. There's no need to yell at me for it. He's leaving, and I need to be away from him."

"Why don't you go to our parent's house? They live in the same town as you." It's the logical choice. Hell, they took her in after her divorce until she was able to get back on her feet.

"You know damn well why I won't." I'm ninety percent sure she's crossing her arms over her chest. It's something she's always done when she's mad. After a long pause, she continues, "Never mind. I'll just stay here at the studio. I'm sure someone will lend me a cot for a couple of weeks."

Dammit. I hate when she does things like this because she knows damn well I'm not going to let her stay there. It's not a bad place, but there isn't a shower or an easy way to cook things unless it's in the microwave. "No, don't do that. You can stay here."

"Thank you," she yells into the phone, and I pull mine away from my ear. She's so freaking loud. "You won't even know I'm there."

"Yeah right," I mutter.

"What was that?"

I lean against the counter, resigned to the fact that it's late and I'm not in the mood to wait for food. I grab one of the small sugared flakes from the bowl and pop it in my mouth, crunching loudly. I'm the little brother, I'm allowed to be immature at times. "Nothing. When will you be here?"

"Probably tomorrow. I don't have any clients coming in for portraits so it won't interfere with that." She sighs and I know even though she doesn't completely have all her shit together, she didn't want to call me. "Thank you, Justin. Going to Mom and your dad wouldn't be such a huge deal, but he made it pretty damn clear that he doesn't approve of my career choice. I'm sure he's waiting for me to fail."

"No, he's not," I argue. "He only wants what's best for you."

"Oh, you mean like when he basically forced you to dump that girl in high school because you were too young to be in a committed relationship before leaving for college?" I sucked in a breath and hate that she brought up

Audrey, especially tonight of all nights. "I guess I hit a nerve. You still think about her, don't you?"

All the damn time. She sneaks into my thoughts without me even realizing it. "It's funny that you mention her. I ran into her tonight…literally. Well, she ran into me."

"You're joking."

"I wish I was." I hear her take a breath, ready to launch into a thousand questions, but I don't give her a chance. "I don't want to get into it tonight. Maybe not ever. It's not like I'm ever going to see her again."

"You never know. This could be Fate's way of bringing you back together. Y'all were such a cute couple when you were in high school. At least, it looked that way from the photos." When did she even see those? I hid them in a box in the back of the storage. Forever burying the memories.

"This isn't high school anymore," I argue. "She probably hates my guts for breaking her heart."

"Or maybe she'll see what a fine young man you've become and she'll be willing to give you another chance."

"I'm not going to take your bait. I'm tired and ready to go to bed." Food, or no food. Talking to Corinne is exhausting sometimes.

Luckily, she doesn't push me for more. "I'll see you tomorrow. Goodnight, Baby Brother."

I hate when she calls me that. She isn't even my real sister. Though we are as close as blood relatives. It makes me feel like I'm twelve years old. "Goodnight. Text me when you're heading this way."

"Will do." With those parting words she ends the call, and I'm left wondering what could happen between me and Audrey.

I leave the bowl of cereal on the counter and go back to my room. I wasn't playing when I said I was tired. Pulling back the sheets on my bed, I climb in and plug my phone into the charge. As I close my eyes, my phone vibrates.

Unknown number: Audrey is home safe and sound.
   Justin: Thank you.

That's one less thing I have to worry about. The memory of her running out of the restaurant at the sight of me will haunt me for a while. I must have really messed her up all those years ago. With that last thought, I roll over, pull the covers over me and drift to sleep. Everything that weighed me down today will be waiting for me tomorrow morning.

Chapter Five

Audrey

THE DRIVE to the apartment is quiet. Johnny navigates the streets while Stella sits beside me, forever my rock. It reminds of when we were kids and she was always standing up for me. She has a tendency to act more like an older sister than my cousin. I'm not complaining since it was just me. We're all only children, and I think the closeness we share is exactly like what siblings must feel. At least, that's what I think. I don't really know anyone that has close family. She wraps her arms around my shoulder and gives me a tight squeeze.

"You doing okay?" She whispers in my ear. It feels loud in the silence and I don't know how Johnny didn't hear it from the front seat.

I can only nod my head. I'm not like my cousins. I don't go for those things that they do. I can't take charge the way they can. That could be why dating has never worked for me. For whatever reason, I don't have that drive to want to put myself out there…emotional scars and all. That clearly bit me in the ass when I was in high school. I didn't fight hard enough for my relationship with Justin. It's why he walked away so easily without looking back.

Within minutes we're in front of my apartment building. The streets are empty and Johnny has no problem finding a parking spot in front. He moves to get out of the truck, but Stella places her free hand on his shoulder and shakes her head the tiniest bit to tell him to stay. "I'll call you in the morning to pick me up, or I'll get a car to take me to the hotel."

I'm not sure why they stay in a hotel. I have a guest bedroom. Tiffany does too since Spencer is no longer just her roommate. I get it, though. They want some privacy. It makes me feel like a bitch that I'm actually happy they made that choice. As much as I love them, I don't know that I could handle all the kisses. I'm content with my life. Well, maybe not as content as I should be, but I'm fine as long as I don't have to witness all the stolen kisses and cuddling. If I become a spinster, I think I'd be okay with it. You don't worry about your heart being ripped out of your chest if you're alone. It might be time for me to look into getting a pet. Maybe that will cure the loneliness.

Stella drags me out of the truck and we head to my apartment. As much as upstairs neighbors can be a pain, I love living on the first floor. I open the door and Stella closes it behind us once we're inside. She points to the sofa and says, "Sit."

I know better than to argue with her. There's a reason she made it to the top of the project management team in her previous job. She knows how to go after what she wants and be stern with those that need it. Apparently, I'm the one that needs that tone of voice right now. She disappears into my kitchen and comes back out with the only bottle of wine I have and two glasses. "Now, tell me what happened."

"I told you," I shrug. "I ran into him."

She raises an eyebrow and gives me the same look my mom does when she thinks I'm being mean to Tiffany. "You know that's not what I'm talking about. What happened back then?"

Sighing, I grab the glass of wine she poured me, and lean back into the corner of the sofa. Running into him tonight brought back all that old pain and anger. Pain that after almost three years of dating, he could dump me without a care in the world. Anger that he did it. That he listened to whatever bullshit his father fed him, and decided I was no longer worth fighting for. Then resignation that I wasn't enough. Not for his father, and obviously, not for him.

I tell her everything that happened. How I thought things were great, and he was going to get his own place if his dad kept being a douche. He dumped me right before Christmas with no warning. He just came by my house and told me things weren't working out and left. And then I tell her about how he had his arm around the most popular girl's shoulder two weeks after we went back to school. "That is what really gutted me, Stell. It made me question my entire relationship with him. If he could move on that easily…how important was I to him when we were together?"

"Well, that was kind of a dick move on his part." Stella lifts her glass and takes a drink. I am already on my second glass and Tiffany still isn't here yet. She knows the full story, though. She was there with me drying my tears for more weeks than I care to remember. "And don't ever question your importance. If he was too stupid to see it, that's his problem. Not yours."

I nod in agreement. "You're telling me. I thought we had our entire future planned out, and it all went in flames." It was more than that, though. It was as if my entire world exploded in the blink of an eye.

She sits up and gasps. "Is that why you didn't go to Hilltown when you graduated? I had everything set for you to join me up here and was floored when you said you were going to a local college. I thought I did something to piss you off."

"Yep, that is why. I couldn't stand to even be in the same school as him. And, we would have had a lot of the same classes since we were on the same business track. It was easiest to stay as far away from him as I could."

"It all makes sense now." She leans back into the sofa and pours more wine into her glass. "Now I feel shitty for being so angry at your sudden change of mind."

"Don't be," I sigh. "It wasn't your fault. I was the one who kept things pretty quiet after he dumped me. I didn't want you to feel like you had to come back and take care of me."

"It still sucks though. And you handled Christmas like nothing was wrong. I did find it odd that he wasn't around considering he did as much as he could with the family."

Before I get the chance to respond my front door flies open and Tiffany stumbles through. "Have no fear, the party is here." She's carrying two grocery bags and they are so full they are almost bursting.

I shake my now empty wine glass in the air. "It's too

late for that, little cousin. Stella and I almost finished an entire bottle."

Tiffany laughs as she sets the bags on the floor "Oh Audrey, it's cute you think that's all you're drinking tonight." She picks up a bottle of vodka and a bottle of bloody Mary mix. "This is just a pregame. We literally have the entire night to ourselves no boys, no jobs, and no drama."

That's easy for her to say. Both her and Stella have significant others. They can finish getting me drunk and go home to somebody. I don't get that luxury. Even after they leave, I'll be here. Alone. With only my thoughts to keep me company. "You aren't going home tonight, are you?" I just want to make sure that I have them until morning, and it will be like the old times.

"No, silly." She goes to the kitchen and fills a few glasses with ice to form bringing them back out to the living room. "You get to put up with my sparkling person-ality all night long. It'll be just like old times."

That is what I need more than anything right now, something to feel normal and ground me. "So, should we make drunken wedding decisions?" I need to change the subject. Think about something else for a bit.

"Absolutely," Tiffany screams. "This is going to be amazing."

"I'm beginning to regret this decision," Stella sighs into her bloody Mary. "Just know that whatever y'all pick tonight, I will make you wear. So, if I were you, I wouldn't decide on anything ridiculous."

I look at Tiffany and shrug my shoulders. "She's not serious. She wouldn't make us wear something hideous." My two best friends are exactly what I want tonight. It gets my mind off of running into Justin, and gives me a tiny smidge of normalcy.

It's not long before were giggling and looking at off-the-wall wedding pictures online. This is what I needed. They take the loneliness away and give me something to look forward to.

Chapter Six

Justin

I JOLT UPRIGHT. What was that sound? Something bangs around in the kitchen, and even though I'm confident in my ass-kicking skills, I'm not sure I want to face down someone breaking into my house. I push the comforter aside and slide out of bed as quietly as possible. In all of my years living here, I've never had to deal with an intruder. I'm not going to rush out of my room like a crazy person, though. Whoever is out could be armed, and quite frankly, I don't want to get hurt. Especially after finding Audrey is here.

Tip-toeing to my closet, I open the door and grab the baseball bat. Thank God I never got rid of it after my one stint in the softball league. Now, that I have a weapon, I can confront the person in my house. As quiet as possible, I open my bedroom door, hoping it doesn't squeak. It doesn't, and I slip through.

My feet are silent as I make my way down the hall, bat

raised above my shoulder like I'm about to swing at a pitch. I round the corner and my fridge slams shut. The person in my house turns around and my bat falls to the ground. "What the hell Corinne? I thought someone was breaking in."

"And you think a bat was going to save you?" She rolls her eyes before opening the freezer. "I think you have bigger problems."

Damn it. She messed up my day of sleeping in and woke me up from my dream about Audrey. It was getting good, too. We were back home and doing the things we normally did when we were in high school except, we were adults. "You were supposed to call me before you came in. What time is it anyway?"

She closes the freezer door, and faces me with her hands on her hips. "I didn't want to wake you up. I had to get out of there because he was being annoying. I didn't realize by not calling I'd be welcomed by my brother with a bat." I like that she's never bothered with adding "step" in front of brother. As far as we're concerned, we're siblings, even if we didn't become family until we were adults. "And it's like 7:30, or something."

"Damn, Rin," I groan and rub my hand over my face. "It's too early to be awake. Did you even sleep last night after we got off the phone?" I did, but it wasn't that great deep sleep you're supposed to get into. Dreams of Audrey kept me tossing and turning. Until the one I was in the middle of before waking up, all of them were a loop of what happened at the restaurant last night. Except sometimes I'd run after her, but I'd always wake up before knowing what happened. I should have gone after her. It's too late now, though.

"Not really," she shrugs. "I packed some stuff, tried to fall asleep, and when I couldn't…I hit the road." She scrunches her nose at me and waves her hand in my direction. "You need to get dressed."

I look down. I have on a t-shirt and basketball shorts. There's nothing wrong with what I'm wearing. "Why?" This is the problem with her being an entire year older than me, she thinks she can tell me what to do. I have a love/hate feeling toward having a sibling most days. I think it'd be different if we had grown up together, but we didn't. Today…it's closer to the latter.

"You don't have any food, and I'm hungry."

"How is that my problem? You could have gotten food before you started rummaging through my fridge. I think you should take a nap, and we'll figure food out at a reasonable hour." She's crazy if she thinks she's going to try to boss me around in my own house. That's not how this works. I'm offering her a place to stay until her latest ex gets out of her house. I'm doing this so that she doesn't have to deal with our parents giving her a hard time about her life choices.

She taps her foot against the tile floor. It's the same thing her mom does when she's about to blow up about something. Usually something Corinne has done. I'm the golden child, at least, to her I am. "Nope. You are going to get dressed," she points to my room. "I'm going to get unpacked. Then we're getting something to eat." She shakes her head as she grabs her suitcases. "I don't see how you survive with no food in the house."

"Like everyone else."

"Which is?" She's heading down the hallway to the guest bedroom.

"Takeout. I don't have a ton of time to cook with work,

and I'll have even less time for the next few weeks. It's easier to grab something on the way home."

"That's not going to fly while I'm here. Now, go get ready. We're leaving in thirty minutes."

For someone who is as flighty as she can be, she's sure as hell bossy. I'll do it, though, because now my stomach is growling. I forgot I didn't even get a chance to eat last night.

When Corinne said we were going to get food, I thought she meant we were going to a restaurant. I didn't think she'd drag me to the damn grocery store. She can do this kind of shopping while I'm at work. There's absolutely zero reason for me to be with her. Cooking has never been my strong point. "Why can't we just go somewhere and get food?"

"Because," Corinne shakes her head. "You need actual food in your house. If you keep eating takeout, you're going to get pudgy."

"No, I won't." We're walking into the store and I'm already feeling overwhelmed. Don't get me wrong, I've gone into the store for a few things here and there. Milk, cereal, ramen, and frozen dinners. You know, the basics. But I've rarely come in to get stuff for actual meals.

She continues as if I haven't said a word. "And if you get fat, you won't be able to win Audrey's heart."

That stops me in my tracks, and Corinne runs into my back. "Who said anything about that? I'm not trying to get back with her."

She moves until she's standing by my side instead of behind me. "Your pissy tone since last night says otherwise. Now walk, you're holding up traffic to get into the store."

I move forward and wait for my sister to get a shopping cart. "I'm serious. I didn't even know she was in the area until last night. Besides, I don't have time to try to start, or restart, a relationship. I work long hours and the merger my company is a part of happens this week."

Corinne shakes her head and pushes the cart into the produce section. "I don't see how that's a problem. The fact that you're protesting so much means you still harbor feelings for her. You can have a career and a girlfriend. People do it every single day."

"I don't think you're the most qualified person to give relationship advice." She winces and drops the orange she just picked up. "Sorry, Rin. I didn't mean it like that."

"Yes, you did." She huffs and continues picking out fruits. "I may not have the best track record when it comes to guys, but I'm not scared to follow my heart."

It's my turn to wince. She knows how to go for the jugular. We turn down the next section and she's now putting vegetables in the cart. I'm not scared. Well, not completely, anyway. I didn't end things well with Audrey. If Tiffany is to be believed, I destroyed her heart, and I'm not sure if that's something she can come back from. "Still out of the question. She probably has a boyfriend, and I don't have a way to get a hold of her. Besides, I still don't have time to commit to anything."

"If you say so, Baby Brother." Now we're going down the aisles of food and I watch her throw things into the cart. I don't know what half of it is. Hopefully she plans on cooking. There's no way in hell I know what to do with any of the food. "So, tell me about this merger."

Thank God she's changing the subject, and knows

when to do it. This is something I could talk about for hours. I love my job and what I do. I only wish we had a chance to meet all of the employees at the company we're merging with. The short turnaround made it hard to do, though. Tomorrow will definitely be interesting, and I hope it all goes well.

Chapter Seven

Audrey

THE SMELL of bacon wakes me up. It makes me miss home. Mom used to make it every weekend. Tiffany and I would always fight over the last piece of bacon. My stomach rumbles as I open my eyes. I'm not sure if it's because I'm hungry or hungover. Most likely the latter. Drums are pounding a steady rhythm in my head, and I could murder my cousins for pumping all that alcohol into my system last night.

I roll out of bed and grab my robe off the back of the door. As I make my way to the kitchen, I start a mental list of everything I need to get done today. Well, assuming my cousins leave at a decent time that is. Otherwise, I'll be digging through the back of my closet trying to find something to wear. The company merger takes place tomorrow and I don't really want to make a bad impression with the new bosses.

Stella and Tiff are sitting at the table when I walk into

the kitchen. Johnny is at the stove cooking. "Good morning, Sunshine," they yell in unison.

The sound reverberates in my skull, and I lift a hand to smooth it away. "Can you bring it down a notch?" My voice is barely above a whisper, and even that is too loud. "How did you get talked into cooking?"

Johnny doesn't turn to answer me, completely focused on his task. "I was going to pick y'all up for brunch, but Stella said you were still passed out. So, I asked her what you had in the fridge and bought some things on my way over." He pauses his stirring to shoot a glance my way. "Besides, with these two, you likely wouldn't have had an edible meal."

He's not lying. Neither one of them can cook to save their lives. Tiffany's mom didn't teach her since she was always eating at my house. And Stella, I don't know what her excuse is. My uncle is a great cook. She can bake, but actual food...she burns to a crisp. "Hey," Stella gasps. "That's not fair. We would have bought something and had it delivered. We're not monsters."

Pulling out an empty chair, I plop into it. I fold my arms on the table and lay my head on top. "How are you feeling?" Tiff's mouth feels like it's right next to my ear. She doesn't need to be this close.

"Like death," I groan, trying, and failing at keeping my voice at a reasonable level. "I drank so much last night." I lift my head about an inch and glare at the two of them. "How are y'all functioning already?" If I hadn't smelled food, my ass would still be in bed, hiding under my blankets.

Tiffany snorts. "You realize I drink a lot, right? Every time Spence and I see Crooked Halo, we end up drinking.

It's part of what we do." She takes a drink of her coffee and sets the cup on the table.

Stella shrugs her shoulders. "I work in a bar most days. Angie is always getting me to try new drinks."

"Who would have thought you would be adventurous," I joke with Stella. "You used to drink around the same amount as me."

Our older cousin scoffs. "I don't think that's true at all. My weakness has always been wine." She waves away the current conversation. "Do you at least feel better emotionally?"

As much as I want to say yes, it wouldn't be the truth. As shitty as I feel right now, I'm grateful my cousins were there for me last night and gave me a chance to drown my sorrows. But...it doesn't stop thoughts of Justin from creeping in. Stella will go back to Asheville and Tiff be will wrapped up in Spencer, leaving me alone with my memories of the boy I used to love. I don't want to give them a reason to worry, though. "Yeah, I'm better. Well," I laugh, "aside from feeling like I'm dying." I push back from the table and sneak to the counter where Johnny is putting the cooked bacon. "I just hope I don't run into him anytime soon." Or, at all. I snatch a piece of bacon from the plate. Johnny tries to sway my hand away, but he's too slow.

"I don't think you'll have to worry about that," Johnny says while flipping the bacon.

My eyes go wide and Stella slowly turns around in her chair until she's facing her fiancé. "How do you know that?" When he doesn't answer, she leaves her chair and marches toward him like a woman on a mission. "What did you do?"

He has the good sense to back away from the stove. Not that Stella would do anything rash, but she can be terrifying when she's pissed off. I grab the tongs out of his hand before he gets too far. There's no reason to let the bacon burn. I'll probably need it after whatever bomb he's about to drop.

He's almost to the living room when he finally speaks, hand raised in the air in surrender. "I text him last night after I dropped y'all off."

"You did *what*," Tiff screeches. "You are not allowed to talk to the enemy." The chair almost topples to the floor as she stands. "How do you even have his number?"

My hand is frozen mid-air. The sizzling bacon in the pan momentarily forgotten. I need to know the answer to this, but I'm terrified to turn around. I don't want anyone to see the panic that must be etched onto my face. I'm almost certain Stella has her hands on her hips with a scowl on her face. If he actually somehow knows Just, I will be mortified.

"Calm down, Tiffany," Johnny sighs. "I don't know him. He gave his number after all of you hightailed it out of the restaurant."

"And you called him?" I can hear the accusation in Stella's voice and her foot tapping a steady, irritated rhythm on the floor. If there is one thing my cousins are, it's loyal. If someone gets on one of our shit lists, they are on all of ours.

I turn off the stove and pull the last of the bacon out of the pan. It's crispy and almost black. Johnny will be getting those pieces. I need to see his response now. If only to put my own mind at ease.

"No, I sent him a text." He throws his hands in the air. "What was I supposed to do? He asked me to let him know that Audrey was okay." He nods toward me and sags his shoulders under his soon to be wife's stare. "He seemed sincere."

"Easy," Tiffany slaps her hand on the table. "You tell him to fuck off and go on about your night. He lost his right to know anything over a decade ago."

"How can you say that?" Johnny argues. "Y'all helped me when I screwed up with Stella." He has a point, loathe as I am to admit it. I swear watching the three of them argue is like watching a ping pong match. And even more frustrating, they are talking about me like I'm not even in the same room.

"That was different," Tiff starts her argument.

I cut her off. "You didn't give him my number or anything, did you?" That's the only thing I need to know. Not that I haven't wondered about him over the years, but thinking about him, and him having a way to contact me are two different things.

"No," he scoffs. "I'm not an asshole. Y'all act like he did something horrible." He pauses for a second. "He didn't, did he? If he ever laid a finger on you, I'll text him again and then kick his ass."

"No," my laugh is soft and sad. "Nothing like that. He was my first love and heartbreak. It's just hard seeing him after all these years."

"Good," Johnny nods. "I didn't want to end up in jail." I love that he's protective over all of us. He's the big brother we never had, and I'm happy he'll officially be part of the family soon.

"Please," Stella scoffs. "You act like you would actually fight him. If anything, you would have a heavily worded conversation with him and be done with it."

"I mean," he shrugs. "If that's all it takes then it's not a bad thing."

I roll my eyes and rush toward Johnny, wrapping my arms around him. "Thank you for looking out for me." Stepping away, I look at the three most important people in my life, aside from my parents. "Seriously, I appreciate y'all being defensive on my behalf, but I'll be okay. I just hope to never see him again."

"That shouldn't be too hard," Tiffany says as she walks to the cabinet to get a plate. "It took you over five years for it to happen this time. Maybe it won't happen for another five."

"You realize you just jinxed me, right?" I grab my own plate and fill it up before sitting at the table. "I don't have time to focus on it, though. Tomorrow is a big day and I need to get everything ready to go so I have a decent start to the week."

"Johnny, why don't you come back in a few hours to pick me up." Stella says as she takes a bite of bacon. She doesn't phrase it as a question. She's demanding it and if he knows better, he'll say okay and go on about his business.

"Why?" He cocks his head to the side like a confused puppy. "Our hotel is on the opposite side of the city. It doesn't make sense to go there, then come back here, only to go back to the hotel to get our things."

"Well, you can get our things in the truck before you pick me up." She nods toward the bottles of wine and liquor in the living room. "Tiffany and I are going to stay and help Audrey clean up. It's not fair for us to make a mess then leave her to pick up after us."

"Um," Tiff raises her hand. "I didn't sign up for this. I don't even like cleaning."

"Too bad," Stella gives her a stern look that stops her

from arguing. "Just because we're grown doesn't mean we stop doing the things our parents instilled in us."

"I guess." Tiffany crosses her arms and pouts. "But," she perks up. "Only if we can help her choose her outfit for tomorrow. We have to make sure she wows the new bosses."

Oh God, no. Anything but that. Tiffany will have me showing off all kinds of skin that is anything except professional. "I don't know." Seriously, cleaning the apartment from top to bottom on my own is preferable to letting my younger cousin dress me.

Stella laughs. "It'll be fine. It's not like I'll let her pick something you aren't comfortable wearing. While we want you to capture their attention, that won't happen if you have clothes you hate."

They aren't going to let it go. They are like a dog with a bone, and it would be in my best interest to let them do their worst. Besides, how will they know if I decide to wear something else. I can always change after whatever picture they demand. It means I'll have to get up earlier, but so be it. I'll allow them to do their little makeover. Their chatter might just be the only thing to keep my mind off Justin. I fear the more I think about him, the more likely I'll run into him. Not that I believe in all that woo woo stuff with thinking things into existence. But I don't want to take my chances. "Fine. Just know that I'm putting the two of you to work. There's a lot I want to get done before tomorrow. I'm not sure if I'll be able to get to anything else for the rest of the week. Who knows what the new bosses are going to throw at us."

Both Stella and Tiffany rub their hands together like they are evil geniuses. Maybe I should be scared after all.

Chapter Eight

Justin

"ARE YOU LEAVING WITHOUT BREAKFAST?" Corinne asks.

Shit. I didn't even see her there. She's such a weirdo. Who the hell sits that quietly in a dimly lit kitchen at six in the morning? "Um, I'll grab something on the way." Maybe that will get her off my back. At least, for today. It's something I know she won't let me get away with for long. Not if the amount of groceries she made me buy yesterday says anything.

"Sit down," she points to the chair across from her. "I already started some biscuits in the oven. I'll cook up some sausage and eggs to make a couple of sandwiches for you."

I take a couple of steps toward the door, hoping she won't see me. It's nothing against her. I only want to get to the office as soon as I can. It's a new building and I need to time the commute. Plus, I need to pump myself up for whatever today is going to bring. It's always a toss-up with how you're going to connect with new co-workers. Or, in my case, employees.

My step sister doesn't miss a beat. "I said sit. You need to start making time for eating something before you leave. It's not healthy to constantly be eating on the go."

"And eating fatty, greasy food at home is better?" I point to the frying pan she pulls out of the cabinet. I honestly don't remember the last time I even used that thing.

"It's better than worrying about getting some sort of food on that expensive ass suit you're wearing. Now take off your jacket, grab a glass of orange juice and sit down."

"When did you become so bossy?" I do what she says, though. There's no way she'll let me out of this house if I don't eat whatever she's cooking. She doesn't care if I'm late or not.

"When I started dating men that didn't know how to be an adult." Her voice is filled with frustration and I want to tell her it's her own fault, but that will start a fight.

I grab a glass out of the cabinet and the orange juice out of the refrigerator. As much as I loathe her ordering me around, I might actually eat a bit healthier. Maybe her visit won't be so bad. I only hope it doesn't turn into a permanent one. I love her, I do. But if she's meddling in my diet, there's no telling what else she will push herself into. I know it's killing her that I'm not doing anything about the whole Audrey situation. I could have sent that guy a text asking for a way to get a hold of her. Hell, I almost did. But that's creepy and I'm not about to do that. Not to her. She deserves so much more than that after the way I treated her.

While I wait for her to finish cooking, I take a seat at the table and pull out my phone. The calendar is going to be my best friend today. There is meeting after meeting scheduled. It's how the higher ups decided to introduce us to the different departments. I think it's ridiculous. We should have met them before the merger even took place. I don't get to make those calls, though. One day, I will. And I'll do things drastically different.

I'm so lost in my thoughts on company domination that I don't notice Corinne has set a plate down in front of me until she starts talking. "Are you nervous about today?"

How could she even know that? I do my best to keep any sort of emotion hidden and tucked away. Emotions portray weakness. It's something I finally learned dealing with my dad. If I acted like his bitching didn't affect me, then he'd stop...eventually. "Not really," I shrug. If I don't let on that I'm okay, she'll badger me about it until I leave. "It's just another day at the office."

"But it's a new office." She lifts her sausage biscuit to her mouth. "New things are typically terrifying."

"It's not that big of a deal. The only difference is there will be new faces. All I have to focus on is learning their names." I take a bite of my food and wait for the next question she has.

"You mean you take the time to learn everyone's name? Is that normal?"

"I like to think so. Not everyone does it, though. They'll get the name of the few people that they'll work with directly and not bother with anyone else."

"That seems very impersonal." Her mouth twists in disgust. Knowing people on a personal level is why she's grown so much as a photographer. People spill their stories to her without a second thought. I think that's why we get along so well. We don't stick to one group of people. We like to get to know everyone. It's also why I never had many enemies when I was in school.

"It is. You can't build trust with your fellow employees if you don't even know their names." I glance at my phone, noting the time. If I don't get going soon, I won't be able to do the car pep talk I started years ago.

"So true." She checks out my plate to make sure I'm eating. "Do you mind if I keep the extra key while I'm here? I kind of want to get out and explore the city, maybe take some photos."

"You plan on being the best photographer in all of Texas?"

She laughs. It's loud and boisterous. Something that isn't heard often in this house unless some of my co-workers are over for a night of football. "How else am I supposed to dominate the photography game?"

Finishing my breakfast, I grab my phone and stand up. "While I'd love to see you take over the world, I need to get to work. I'm pushing it on timing how long it takes to get there on a normal day." I stop where she sits and give her a quick hug. "I'll be home at some point today. I'm not sure when since our last meeting starts at four thirty."

"Have a good sort of first day," she grins, and if I didn't know any better, she's hiding something. It's the way the corner of her mouth lifts up slightly higher than the other. What isn't she telling me? "I'll have dinner set aside for you whenever you get here."

I swear she's trying to fatten me up. I'm going to end up rocking a dad bod and I don't even have any kids. The only thing I can do is shake my head. When she goes back home, I'll be hitting the gym a lot more than I do now. "See you later, Sis."

~

My car is already warming up in the bright summer sun. The way it beats down on me makes me wish I could dress casual for my job. I need to be in my new office in fifteen minutes. You can do this. It's just like any other job. Technically, it's still the same job, just in a different building. The people you'll be managing won't hate you. Put one foot in front of the other and learn their names. That's all you have to do.

Now that my talk is out of the way, I turn off the car and open the door. It's even warmer out here thanks to a lack of air conditioning. Normally, I'd park in the garage attached to the building, but I don't have a parking badge yet, so the open parking lot a block down will have to be good enough. I grab my jacket off the passenger seat and close the door behind me before pressing the lock button. One foot in front of the other, I walk to the building I'll now be spending so much time at.

Cold air blasts as I enter the lobby and the man at the desk looks up when my shadow passes over him. "Hi, how can I help you?"

"Hello, today is actually my first day in this building. I'm part of the merger with TK. I still need to get my badge."

"I can get that started for you right now. I just need your ID." I pull it out of my wallet and hand it over to him. He scans it into his computer and hands it back. "Now, if you'll step around here, I can get your photo."

It's the same thing we did at the other office. We had part of one of the buildings and I'm no stranger to this song and dance. I stand against the wall and he takes a couple of pictures. "I'll have this ready for you around lunch."

"Thank you," I wave at him as I make my way to the elevator. "I'll see you then."

It feels like forever until an elevator door opens up and I step inside. The door is about to close when someone rushes in yelling, "Wait."

Hold on, I know that voice. I look down and none other than Audrey is standing in front of me wide-eyed. "What are you doing here?"

"You have got to be fucking kidding me," she backs out of the elevator and starts running back through the lobby. Something about Tiffany being a bitch. She's not wrong there at times.

Why does this woman continue to run away from me? This time I'm not going to stand here in stunned silence. I chase after her.

Chapter Nine

Audrey

THESE HEELS ARE impossible to run in. Is Justin stalking me? I can't think of another reason he'd be here…in my building. "I'm going to murder Tiffany," I mutter. This never would have happened if she wouldn't have said anything. She wished this into existence.

"Audrey, wait." Shit, he's following me. I'm not sure what to do. I could duck into one of the other buildings, or stores, but I know he'd come in right behind me. I'll round the block and make my way back to the car. Calling in sick is my best option until I figure out why he's here.

I round the corner, and keep going as far as my feet can take me. If this is going to become a habit, I'm really going to have to start working out. This is becoming ridiculous. I should not have to run this much in such a short period of time. One day I'll understand why people think it's fun. Today is not that day.

I'm so lost in my thoughts that I don't hear Justin close the distance between us. A hand grabs my arms and pulls me to a stop. "Why," he gasps. "Are you." Another gasp. "Always running from me?" He lets go of me only to put his hands on his knees and bend over, trying to catch his breath.

I could run again, but let's be real, I'm just as out of breath as he is. Never in a million years will I show it, though. Instead of answering him right away, I stand up straight and take a few deep breaths. Anything to make it easier not to gasp while I'm talking to him. It seems like that's the only way I'm going to put an end to running into him. "Why were you at my job?"

There. Answer a question with a question. Stella would be so proud. He doesn't have to know that underneath my false bravado, I'm quaking. Terrified of how he'll answer. That he's purposefully seeking me out and this isn't a coincidence. I'm not sure how I'll react either way. On the one hand, it'll mean he still does care. Or, at least wants to see how I'm doing after all these years. On the other…I can't believe that's it. If Tiffany were here, she would say its Fate's way of pushing us together, even though she hates his guts. She'll probably feel differently if that's the case in the end. Please, don't let it be.

That gets his attention, though. He's still breathing hard. His chest moving up and down, his shirt damp from sweating while trying to catch up with me. He's much more defined now than he was when we were eighteen. Shouldn't that mean he's in shape and can handle the running? "Wait, you work there?"

Oh snap. He didn't know I work there. What other reason can he have for being there. I don't remember anyone saying anything about there being new employees with the merger. Unless… "Please tell me you aren't with the company joining us?"

Justin stands ramrod straight. "If I say yes, are you going to run again?"

I take a few steps back, the instinct to run higher than ever before. I'll never be able to escape his presence now. Should I run? Yes, undoubtedly. Will I? No. There is no energy left to do any sort of physical activity. "No, I won't run. But how did you not know that I worked there?"

His shoulders sag. My promise not to jet visibly relaxes him. "There wasn't much time to do anything. And they didn't give us the list of employees already here."

"That's kind of stupid." I want to reel the words back in as soon as I've said them. He could have been one of those people that made the decision.

"I agree." He surprises me by the answer and even seems a little pissed that he didn't get a list. "I wanted to meet as many people as possible before today. It helps with morale and doesn't feel like a complete takeover."

"But that's essentially what you're doing right?" I tap my foot against the concrete waiting for his response. "Y'all were all brought on as management. You may even be my boss. Wouldn't that be a conflict of interest?"

He shrugs his shoulders. "Maybe? But that's beside the point. We came on to make the company you work for better. They weren't exactly in great shape and came to us to help fix it. Though, don't tell anyone that. I don't think y'all know exactly how bad off y'all were before we stepped in."

They didn't. I assumed everything was fine and we were joining to help another company. Obviously, I was wrong. So much for transparency in the work place. I mean, I understand why. People would have freaked out, but some sort of communication would have been nice.

"Well, I guess the only thing to do now is go back to the office and see where we end up."

"Why did you run the other day?" His question is completely out of left field and takes me by surprise...again.

"You, Justin. You seem to be the only reason I revert to cardio on sight." It's hard for me to admit that, and I can't believe I just did. He seems to bring out the best and worst in me.

He takes a step closer, his hands up as if he's placating a scared animal. He's not totally off. "That doesn't answer why."

It doesn't and I'm one hundred percent okay with that. "I think I should probably get back to the office. I'm sure my boss is wondering where I am."

Without giving him a chance to argue, I brush past him and head toward the building. I don't look back to see if he's following. That point is moot now that I know he's not stalking me, and is working with me. Hell, I may even be under his supervision. I wonder if it's too late to consider a career change. Or, maybe even a new job.

I haven't seen, or heard from, Justin since I came back to the building. Good. I don't have the mental capacity to deal with him right now. The only thing I need to know is if he will be one of my direct bosses. If so…that will suck. Looking for a new job will suck even more. I love working here, and even though my emotional wounds from him are old, they still hurt. I don't want to deal with him on a day-to-day basis.

My phone vibrates with a message just as my computer

dings with an alert. I check the work notification first. Looks like we have a meeting in a few hours. Too bad it isn't voluntary. I'm pretty sure I know what we'll be going over. Now time for my phone. It's the group text with my cousins.

Tiff: So how did the new bosses like your outfit?

Me: I'm going to kill you.

Stella: They hated it that much.

Tiff: I don't see how. It was perfect.

Me: Never mind about the damn outfit. You wished me seeing Justin into existence.

Tiff: No, I didn't. I said I hope you don't run into him again.

Me: Which one hundred percent jinxed me. He's part of the merger.

Stella: Oh shit.

Tiff: Maybe it won't be so bad. He may be over one of the other departments.

Me: You better hope so.

Stella: There's nothing you can do about it now. Finish out your work day and let us know when you find out more. We'll figure it out.

Stella is right. It doesn't make it less frustrating, though. I'll just power through my tasks until the meeting. We're bound to find out more. I'm just crossing my fingers he's not directly over me. How embarrassing will it be having to report to the man who broke your heart?

Chapter Ten

Justin

THERE AREN'T VERY **many meetings** left for the day. I've yet to see Audrey in any of the ones from this morning, which means there's a higher chance that she'll be one of the employees under my supervision. I don't want that to be the case. I'd be lying if I said I wasn't nervous about seeing her, or the fact that seeing me causes her to run like her life depends on it. I'm shuffling through their merger information for the fifth time. I know these words like the back of my hand. Right now, though, I can't remember them for the life of me. The words blur together and I shake my head in an attempt to clear my vision.

"Is everything okay?" Carter asks. He sits down next to me at the long conference table. He's the only person that I can count on. We were hired on at Bolder & Barnes around the same time and have been buddies ever since.

I run a finger between the collar of my shirt and neck. The closer it gets to the next meeting, the harder it is to breathe. "Yeah, I'm fine," I clear my throat and reach for my bottle of water.

He laughs, and I wince the tiniest bit. "You can't bull-shit a bullshitter. You've been tense all day, but I didn't want to say anything. Now, you're sweating and I know something is up." I open my mouth to speak, and he shakes his head. "Aside from new employee nerves. This is something else."

Should I tell him about Audrey working here? I gave him a few details yesterday, but didn't say much. Not enough for him to know that there's a history between the two of us. One that goes back over a decade. "You know how I was telling you about that girl?" He nods his head, and motions his hand for me to continue. Fuck. I feel like a teenager defending my choices to my father all over again. "Well, I dated her in high school. More like I broke her heart."

"Okay, and what does that have to do with how you're acting right now?"

"Well," I clear my throat again. This time it has nothing to do with being thirsty. "She also works here."

"Like in the building?" He waves his hand. "Do you realize how many companies are in this place?"

"No, she works in this company. The one we're here to fix and keep an eye on." I pause waiting for his reaction. I'm usually the levelheaded one in this duo, but now is obviously not that time.

"Damn, man." He lets that sink in for a few moments. The chatter outside the conference room is the only back-ground noise. "You aren't trying to pursue her, are you?"

A chuckle escapes from me. "Dude, she hates my guts. Even if I really wanted to, she'd shut that shit down pretty quickly." I mean what I'm saying, but she's already gotten under my skin again. Corinne was right. Running into Audrey and chasing after her this morning is proof of that. If I didn't care, I would have headed straight to work. But no, I had to run after her. I really wish she would have been honest about why she ran from me. But she didn't give me an answer. Not really.

"Then you have nothing to worry about," Carter shrugs and leans back in his chair. "Want to grab a drink when we're done for the day?"

I weigh my options. On one hand, I'd love to go out for drinks after this stressful day. On the other…Corinne would kill me if I stayed out even later after she made dinner. "I probably shouldn't. Corinne is making dinner."

"Your sister is in town?" He grins and I don't like it at all. "We can always have drinks at your place. I know you keep it pretty well stocked." He's not wrong. I have a full bar set up, but I rarely touch it. If I want a drink, I go out with him.

"You are not going to try anything with my sister. She's coming out of yet another shit relationship, and doesn't need you trying to jump in her bed."

"Since when do you have a sister?" The sound of her voice makes me straighten my spine. Is it already time for the next meeting? I check my phone and we still have another ten minutes before people are supposed to come in.

Before I can say anything, Carter vacates his seat, rounds the table and holds out his hand. "You must be the one who hates his guts." He points his thumb in my direction. "I'm Carter."

Audrey's cheeks blush a dark pink. It's nice to see some things never change. She's never been great at handling attention. She takes a deep breath and places her hand in Carter's, "I'm Audrey. I guess you're one of the new guys on the block."

"Yep," he nods. "And if you're here for the next meeting, I'm one of your new bosses."

"I guess that means he is my other one." She nods toward me and I don't miss the disdain she adds to "he".

"Sort of?" Carter phrases it like a question. "He's more like my supervisor. So, I report to him if there are any problems."

Audrey takes a seat as far from me as possible. "So how does this work? Y'all move in and kick out our current management?"

"Actually," I begin, but she cuts me off.

"Sorry, Justin. I was actually speaking to Carter since he's the one I'll be sending reports to." Damn. When did she get so sassy? I think Tiffany and Stella are starting to rub off on her. Or she's trying to make me feel stupid. That's not who she is, though. At least, that's not who she used to be.

Carter mutters "damn" and shakes his head. He's getting a kick out of this. Asshole. He doesn't pay me any mind, though. "I'll be working with your current boss." Carter sits down next to Audrey, and it kills me that she's allowing him to be so close to her and she just met him. I don't care if it's work related. Why won't she let me tell her how it all plays out. "We're not trying to replace anyone. The whole point of us being here is helping the company you work for survive and thrive. We," he waves his hand between me and him, "are the best of the best in the area. We have multi-million-dollar accounts that we bring with us."

Audrey snorts, and Carter stops in his tracks. "Sorry,"

she laughs again. "It's just that your clout," she adds finger quotes to the words. "Doesn't mean anything to me. I'm here to do my job. As long as I know my job is safe, and I have little to no interaction with him, then I'm good."

"I think we're good, then." Carter leans back in his chair. "Have you ever thought about management? I like how straightforward you are. You cut straight through the bs."

"Nope. That's more my cousin's expertise." She's blushing again. Not only does attention make her uncomfortable, so does compliments. It's the one thing I made sure to give her every day when we were teens. I wanted her to know that even though she was sometimes overshadowed by her cousins, she was strong and deserved to be seen as well.

"Is your cousin as feisty as you?" Carter asks.

Okay, I have to step in now before he makes an ass of himself. "Calm down, Romeo. From what I saw the other night Stella is one hundred percent taken."

Audrey glances at me before turning her attention back to Carter. "She's actually engaged."

"Congrats to her," Carter says. "You should come have drinks with us after work."

I never agreed to have drinks especially since he has his eyes on my sister. Luckily, I don't have to shut that shit down because Audrey answers, "Sorry, I have plans."

Nobody has a chance to say anything else because the rest of her department shows up for the meeting and take their seats around the table. I stand to give someone my seat. I do my best talking when I'm on my feet. Audrey is glaring at me while I wait for everyone to be seated. All that does is make me want to know the reason. I mean, I know, but I want her to tell me. I want her to show me the spunk she just showed Carter. Even if it makes her uncomfortable.

Chapter Eleven

Audrey

WHY DOES he have to stand at the front of the conference room looking hot while I'm sitting here pissed because he is in my space once again. That last half of Senior year was miserable. It was impossible not to run into him because our graduating class was less than a hundred. It seems I can't escape him now, either. And why am I finding him attractive? I mean, I have eyes, but remember the way he dropped me and moved on like I meant nothing still stings. He was my forever. At least, I thought he was.

"Audrey," Luke, my coworker, nudges my arm with his elbow. "The meeting is over."

"Sorry, I guess I zoned out." Or maybe I was stuck in my head and couldn't snap out of it long enough to realize the meeting was over.

He laughs and shakes his head. "Must have been some daydream." He scoots out of his chair and offers his hand to help me out of mine. I don't take it, but he's used to that and doesn't get offended. He likes to be a gentleman.

"Want to grab drinks after work? Or is your cousin dragging you off to another show?"

"No," I sigh. "Thank God. It seems Crooked Halo is playing out of state right now so I have a reprieve." I push out of the chair and make sure my phone is in my pocket. "I'm good with drinks. But I don't want to stay out too late. Stella is supposed to video chat with us about our bridesmaid dresses."

"Sounds good." He heads toward the door and waves. "I'll catch ya at quittin' time."

I'm about to follow Luke out of the room when I hear Justin call my name. "Audrey." Luke had me distracted long enough that I completely forgot him and Carter are still in the room. "Can I talk to you for a second?"

I'm not sure I have much of a choice since he's part of management now. "Sure, what do you need?" Carter shrugs his shoulders and leaves the room as fast as he can.

"I thought you said you have plans tonight?" He crosses his arms over his chest, and I don't miss the way his biceps fill out the button up shirt he has on. He was tall and lanky when we were in high school. But now…he's the man I always envisioned him to be with bigger muscles. And, if I'm not mistaken, jealousy crosses his face. He's not even looking directly at me. He's staring at the door where Luke passed through minutes ago. This is going to be fun.

"I do," I motion toward the door. "With Luke."

"Yeah, but you literally just made those plans. You couldn't have known he was going to ask you out before the meeting started." His eyes meet mine, and they're asking a question that's quite frankly none of his business.

"It's a normal thing. We go have drinks at least once a week. Why are you so concerned?" I lean against the table and wait for his response. Wanting him to come right out with the question. It's the only way he's going to get an answer from me. Not that he deserves one. What I do is none of his business.

"Are you…," he begins then changes course completely. Coward. "Are we going to be able to work together without any issues? I can try to transfer to payables if it's going to be a problem."

My head snaps back at the offer. Who knew he would attempt something so considerate it? Maybe he's changed after all this time, and stopped letting his dad run his life. "When did you get a sister?"

He taps his fingers against his arms, and for a second I don't think he's going to answer me. After all, I didn't confirm that working together was going to be a problem. "Not long after I left for college. Dad met someone and they got married a few years later. Corinne is barely older than me, but she's pretty awesome."

Wow. His dad got remarried. You would think I'd know that considering I was still in town when all that went down. Or that my parents would have told me since I avoided him at all costs. If I went to a store and he was there, I'd enter a different aisle or leave the store altogether. "That's good. I'm glad y'all are one happy family."

Not going to lie, it sucks that his dad was so quick to judge me and get me as far from him as possible, but he jumped into a marriage fairly quick if you ask me. "Don't be like that, Audrey." He reaches one hand toward me and I step back, leaving it hanging in mid-air.

"It's fine." I start toward the door, ready to leave this conference room behind. "As long as we don't have to interact on a daily basis, I think we'll be able to work together just fine." I'm out of the door before he can say anything else. Everything will be okay. It has to be. As much as I don't want to work with Justin, I have no desire to look for another job. I like the people I work with for the most part. I'm not going to let him run me out of my job.

Sports are on every television in the bar. It's a hole in the wall place a couple of blocks from the office. It's close enough to walk to when we get off. A lot of my coworkers come here after a long day of dealing with clients. The few tables here are taken, and it's too warm to sit on the patio. At least in this outfit. My legs would be chafing before we got our drink order if we sat out there.

A trio leaves the bar and we take advantage. Luke sits on the barstool to my right. We're regulars and the bartender doesn't even ask us what we want. She knows, and I appreciate that. Even though I don't drink much, today definitely calls for it. I looked over my shoulder constantly to make sure Justin wasn't looking for me or watching me. Yeah, that makes him sound creepy. He's not, but I wouldn't put it past him to try to find out if Luke and I are dating.

Hannah sets our drinks down in front of us and I take a long drink before placing it on the bar top. Luke turns toward me. "Tell me if this is too personal, but I have a gut feeling you know that Justin guy."

My head falls back and I groan. "Yeah, I know him. Well, I used to." I take another drink.

"I'm sensing there's a story there." When I say nothing, he leans forward the tiniest bit. "Are you going to spill? Or, am I going to have to make up scenarios?"

He's as bad as my cousins. But aside from them, he's

one of my closest friends. We tried the dating thing once and it was weird. He's like a sibling to me, and if I don't tell him, he's going to bug the hell out of me.

"Wow." He takes a long pull of his beer and rests an elbow on the sticky bar. "He just dumped you with a bullshit excuse. That's harsh."

"Tell me about it." I let out a breath. "At eighteen, I thought it was the end of the world. He was my first love. Time should have made that feeling go away, right? It almost hurts as much now as it did then."

"There's two possible reasons for that." I roll my eyes at him. Here we go. He's a lot like me. He likes to solve problems, but never his own. I think that's why we get along so well. We offer the other a different perspective. "Just hear me out." He waits for Hannah to give us another drink before he begins. "One, you don't have closure. He dumped you out of the blue and you never really recovered. Two…you still love him."

"I really dislike you right now." There may be a bit of truth to both of them. Hell, I haven't seriously dated a guy since him. When he left for college, I would fantasize about him coming back to me. Without his father watching his every move, I just knew he'd come sweep me off my feet. The longer it didn't happen, the more I realized I didn't mean much to him. It didn't stop me from carrying a torch for the asshole, though. I've measured every man to the guy I loved with my whole heart and they've all been lacking.

"Because I'm telling you what you don't want to admit?" He nudges me with his shoulder. "I'm one hundred percent fine with that. We need to see if he still has a thing for you. You never know. He may not be the same douchebag he was the night he broke up with you. It's been a decade; he might have changed."

"That's a horrible idea." Luke starts to argue, but I cut him off. "He's our boss for crying out loud. I can't go down that hole. I'm sure there's something in our employee handbook about that sort of relationship."

A grin takes over his face. "I'm going to look through it to double check. Then…it's on."

"Ugh, it's a horrible idea." My phone rings and I grab it out of my bag. "Oh shit. I lost track of time." Swiping my phone, I answer the video call. Stella and Tiffany are squinting at me trying to figure out where I am. "Hey, guys."

"Are you in a bar? How the hell are we supposed to look at the horrible dresses the two of you picked out when you're around a bunch of people." Stella whines.

I mute the phone. "Sorry, Luke. I need to go."

"No worries," he waves his hand before throwing some bills on the bar, "I'll drive you home while you talk to your cousins then get a ride back to my car."

"You don't have to do that."

"It's fine." I reach in my bag for my wallet. "Put that away. Tonight, was my treat. You had one fucked up day."

He's not lying. It was the most stressed out I've been in years. "Thanks." I unmute my phone and we walk out of the bar. I'm sure once I'm alone my cousins will bombard me with questions about how the rest of my day went. But I needed this tonight with Luke. I'm also interested in what the handbook says about dating. Not that I'm going to pursue anything with Justin. The only thing I'll find down that path is heartache.

Chapter Twelve

Justin

"You know you look like a stalker, right?" Carter claps me on the back and leans on the door of my office.

"I don't know what you're talking about." I do, but I'm going to play dumb. I thought it would be easy working with her. Guess I'm a moron for letting that into my head. We don't interact with each other. It's been three weeks and she comes in to drop reports off on my desk before hightailing it out of my office.

"How many times have you gone out there to make copies?" I answer with a shrug. "There's no way you need that many copies of a report that you can print off your computer." He points toward the corner of the table along the back wall. "On the printer that is right here in your office. You have it bad."

I lay my head down on my desk. Why is this so damn hard? I thought about her over the years, but it wasn't anything like it is now. I feel consumed by her...the same way I felt when we were in high school and she was my universe. "I know. I don't know how to make it stop, though." When I lift my head, he's staring out the door.

"That's easy, friend." He walks back to my desk and points at me. "That's easy. You get off your ass and go talk to her." Carter shakes his hand and tries to pull me up from my seat. "Seriously, dude, it's the only way you're going to solve anything. As far as you know, she's having the same thoughts as you."

I pull away from him. "I doubt it. She's all buddy, buddy with that Luke guy." My stomach churns at the thought of him touching her. For fucks sake. I don't get jealous. Especially when I'm not even with the girl. How is that even possible?

"Have you asked her if she's dating him? That would go a long way in dealing with this macho man bullshit you have going on."

I haven't. I was hoping that day after the meeting she would tell me. Hell, I begged her with my eyes. A look that worked so many times when we were younger. She didn't, though. Instead, she changed the subject and wanted me to feel that pang of hurt that she might have moved on. "No. It's not really my business. Not only because I'm her boss, but also because I don't have that right. Not after the way I ended things when we were in high school."

Now that he's given up on trying to force me to talk to the woman I let get away, he sits on the edge of my desk. "How did all that go down? I mean, I'm not trying to start a gab session, but you've never really said exactly what happened."

Rubbing a hand over my face, I exhale. "It's a long story. But the highlights...my dad pretty much hounded me until I did it. At the time his reasoning made sense.

Now, though, I think it was one of the biggest mistakes I've ever made."

"Okay, I'm going to need you to spill more than that. That's nothing but a tease. What exactly was your dad's reasoning? Was she a troublemaker in school? Cheated? What? Because from where I'm standing, she's a pretty amazing woman."

Why does it sound like he's fawning over her? Honestly, I think if I didn't have a past with her, he'd be doing everything he could to go on a date with her. "She's so much more amazing than she was in high school. Back then, she'd let people push her around and I, along with one of her cousins, would always stand up for her. It's good to see she has a backbone now." I'm more than likely the reason for that. Or she just grew into the woman she was meant to be.

"And your dad?" Damn, he's really not letting this go. I mean I guess that's what best friends are for. I don't think Corinne even bugged me this much. I need to find out when she's going home. She's driving me as crazy as Carter is with all the Audrey questions.

"He didn't think it was a good idea to go off to college with a girlfriend."

"That's not that uncommon. There's something you're not telling me."

I don't think my stepmom even knows the real reason. I told Corinne not to tell anyone when she finally nagged me enough to tell her. "So, my dad and mom were high school sweethearts. They both went off to college together. Their last year before they graduated, they got pregnant with me. The only problem is...after I was born, Mom decided she didn't want to have the mom life. She met someone else ran away with him as fast as she could leaving me and my dad behind."

Carter whistles and stands. "Damn. But why does he think that would happen to you? He knows not everyone is the same right? I mean he did get remarried."

"I have no freaking clue. I think a lot of it is we reminded him of them. We were inseparable and did everything together. I can count on two hands how many days I went without seeing her when we were teens." And it's true. I spent every moment I could with her outside of school and work. "It was almost obsessive. As much as it broke both of us, maybe it was the right decision. I don't think either of us will ever really know. It's not like we can go back in time."

"Does she know any of this?" He nods to the main area.

"No. I dumped her pretty fast and after a couple of weeks dated a few other people to keep my mind off her. It just made sense because the two of us were intense together. We had our whole future planned out." I'm at a place now where I can appreciate that, but then...it scared me shitless.

"And that is why she dislikes you so much."

"Why?"

"Because you moved on, Man. Do you not watch any movies? She thought she didn't mean anything to you."

Looking back, I did act like a dick. "It wasn't that bad."

"If you say so." He glances out the window to the farm of cubicles again. Laughing he looks back at me before heading to the door. "Now is your chance to talk to her. She's coming this way." Then he leaves. Asshole.

"Here's the report you asked for," Audrey says as she plops the folder on my desk. "Is there anything else you're going to need? I do actually have other work to do besides answering your five thousand questions. I'm not your personal secretary."

Damn, she's got some fire in her veins today. And here I am, emotionally spent from spilling my guts to Carter. If I didn't know better, I'd say he did this on purpose. He wanted me vulnerable so I'd actually do something about this mess with Audrey. "I'm sorry. I don't mean to take up all your time. I only want to know where the company stands so we can see what needs to happen to make it better."

She throws her hands on her hips and it's shocking how much she looks like her mom when she does it. I remember being on the receiving end of that scowl when were teens. Her mom wasn't mad at us often, but she was a stickler for curfew. As long as Audrey was home, I could stay as long as I wanted. I even fell asleep on their couch once and they didn't have any issue with it since Audrey was in her own bed. Her voice pulls me from the memory of much better times. "Well, is that all you need? Like I said, I have stuff to do, clients to call and billings I need to get out."

I wonder if she'd talk to any other boss that way. I'm guessing no because she doesn't like confrontation. Hell, I'm surprised she's confronting me the way she has. It seems like a bad time to ask her about Luke, but I need to know. Maybe it'll stop me from making an ass of myself. "Sort of. I, um, need to ask."

"Ask me what, Justin?" Her hands are no longer on her hips. They've moved down to the edge of her blouse, playing with the ends. It's something she did when she was nervous. At least I know that I'm not the only feeling some sort of way.

"Is there something going on with you and Luke?" There. It's out there and we'll see if she answers me.

She chews on her bottom lip, looking everywhere in the office except at me. Everything in my body is telling me to get up, shut the blinds on my windows and replace her teeth with my lips. She's not out of my system, and never was. Every other woman was a poor replacement for the one person I've wanted since the day I dumped her. Finally, she lets go of her lip, takes a deep breath, and looks me square in the eye. "We're just friends. We have been since we started working here." My shoulders sag and I can feel that weight lifted from me. "Why?"

Okay, I wasn't prepared for that. "I'd rather not get into that on company time. Maybe we can grab a bite to eat after work. Or, just go somewhere to talk?" It's a long shot and I hope she accepts.

"I can't tonight."

"For real, or are you making an excuse?" I need to know if she's just avoiding me.

"No, I really can't. Stella scheduled a dress fitting for me and Tiffany. Apparently, she doesn't trust us to do it ourselves." She looks toward the window that shows parts of the city. "Even though I'm the most responsible one," she mutters under her breath.

It breaks my heart all over again. She's amazing and her cousins have never given her the credit she deserves because she usually goes along with whatever they want with no fuss. "Oh, okay. Just let me know when you're free. I guess you're pretty busy with Stella's wedding."

"Yeah," she scrunches her nose, annoyed. "Actually, Friday night I'm going to see Crooked Halo with Tiffany. She wouldn't take no for an answer and I have to go.

They're pretty decent. I think Tiffany is trying to persuade them to play at Stella's wedding."

"Sounds good." I stand but she backs up toward the door. "I'll, um, meet you after work on Friday."

"I better get back to work." She runs into the chair in front of my desk and stumbles before hurrying out the door.

We have a plan. This is it. I have my chance to explain and to see if she wants to give this another go. Despite how much I've told Carter and Corinne that I don't want her, I can't lie to myself. Working with her is too much. I need her in my life outside the office.

Chapter Thirteen

Audrey

"Tell me again why you invited him?" Tiffany leans against the bar next to me while Spencer is explaining how he got involved with Crooked Halo. She's one hundred percent against this idea. It's why I didn't inform her of my plan. And it's why I didn't let them pick me up like they normally do. Him meeting me here was always an option. But the only way I'm going to find out what he has to say is if he's here. If I came with him, he wouldn't be able to back out.

"He said he wanted to talk about stuff but we couldn't do it at the office." I've already told her this five times since we've been here. She hasn't even had anything to drink so I know that's not the reason. "Besides, maybe it'll bring me closure. Do you know how hard it is working with him?"

"Does he treat you badly at work?" Tiffany turns her glare toward the man in question.

"No, not at all. It's just...I don't know. It's weird seeing him every day. I think most days he's going out of his way to be around me. There's no way he needs all the reports he says he does." For others that might be off putting, but for me, it shows me that he does at least care. In some weird sort of way, anyway. It's those little things. My annoyance is only somewhat of an act. I really do have better things to do. I like it on some masochistic level, though. I get to see him and know that he's as affected as I am. He's not bad to look at, either.

I glance at him now. He's still taller than me and carries himself confidently. I thought he looked amazing in a pair of slacks, but the jeans he changed into before we came to the bar hug him in all the right places. "Stop looking at him like you're going to jump his bones. It's gross." Tiffany pulls my gaze away from him.

"I don't know what you're talking about." He looks good enough to eat. Would it be such a bad thing if we did have sex? It wouldn't be the first time. We weren't exactly innocent when we were teens. It'd be interesting to see what each of us has learned since we've grown up. Not that I have a ton of experience. Dating definitely wasn't a priority when I moved here no matter how much my cousins pushed me to do it. I'm not like Tiff, though. I need to have real, tangible feelings for someone before I hop into bed with them.

"Mhmm." Tiff takes a drink of her whiskey. "You're looking at him the same way I look at Spencer. I know that look well."

I fake gag. "I did not need to know that Tiffany." A shiver runs down my spine. I swear she has no filters. She says whatever she thinks, and I'm rethinking having Justin here. There's no telling what she'll say to him, especially if it's been bottled up all these years.

"Do you not like your drink?" Justin says from behind me, and I jump. "I can get you a water or something else."

"No," I shake my head. "I'm good. I tolerate alcohol much better than I did back in high school."

Tiffany snorts. "You don't have to lie to him. You barely drink unless I'm forcing it on you."

I glare at my cousin and shake my head trying to tell her to shut up. He doesn't need to know that I only drink when I'm upset or nervous. It helps numb whatever is bothering me or lets me speak more than I normally would. "Really, Justin, it's fine. I typically go for the fruity drinks and not the stout ones."

"Give me two seconds," Justin holds up two fingers. "I'll fix that for you."

As soon as he leaves, Tiff raises her eyebrows. "Wow, he's sucking up big time. Whatever he wants to talk to you about is either going to destroy you or land you in his bed."

From where I'm standing, both options suck. Admitting that he still has the power to destroy me is like a slap in the face. And even though ending up in his bed wouldn't necessarily be horrible, it's definitely not something I'm looking forward to since we're just reconnecting. Hell, I don't even have a reason about why he got me all those years ago and then went on with his life as if I never existed. "I'm not gonna let him do either of those things. I won't allow him to have that sort of power over me anymore."

Tiffany almost spit her drink all over me as she laughed. "That is the most full of shit statement I have ever heard. If he no longer had power over your emotions, you wouldn't run every time you see him."

"I work with him, Tiffany. I can't exactly run from him anymore."

"Whatever you say Audrey." She rolls her eyes and strolls away from me just as Justin comes up beside me.

"What was all that about?" He hands me a bright pink drink, and I hope I like this one much better than the last he gave me.

I sigh and shrug at the same time. "It's just Tiffany being Tiffany. You know how that goes."

"Yeah," he chuckles. "She really hasn't changed much after all these years. I figured if anything her temper would've calmed down some."

"Oh no, it's still there. Now it just takes a little bit longer to piss her off," I looked him up and down, "unless you're already on her bad side. Then she's just going to shoot flames at you as much as she can."

"About that," he begins. "I wanted to explain what happened then."

I've already decided I'm going to give him that chance. Now, I need to figure out if I'm going to allow him to do it without me giving him any crap about it. "Oh, you mean when you dropped me like I meant nothing and started dating half the senior class? You mean what happened then?" Yeah, I'm definitely going to give him crap. He turned the last half of my senior year into my own personal hell.

"Dammit, Carter was right," he mutters under his breath.

"Right about what?" The band that is playing before Crooked Halo is beginning to warm up and we are going to lose the chance to hash this out.

He runs a hand on his face and groans. "About how you felt. You would think I would've put two and two together, but apparently, I'm an idiot. Please, don't tell him he was right. I'll never hear the end of it."

But I'm definitely telling him he was right. I knew I liked Carter for a reason. "Let's see how the rest of the evening goes, then I'll decide whether or not I'll keep your secret. So, how about you tell me what happened because from where I was standing everything was perfect and we are ready to set off on our lives together."

"You may want to sit down for this."

Luckily for me, the bar owner always has a table ready for Tiffany and Spencer whenever Crooked Halo plays here. I don't know why, because they never actually sit at it, but it's there just in case. "Follow me."

The instinct to grab his hand and pull him along like I used to when we were teenagers is strong, but my resolve is stronger. I weave between bar patrons until I find the table tucked away in a corner. It's not so far back that you can't see the stage clearly, but it's its own little private paradise for when you need a breather at a concert.

We take our seats and he places his hands on the small circular table. "First off, I want to apologize for how I handle things in high school. I was 18, dumb, scared, and believed my dad had my best interests at heart."

I was right. His dad definitely had something to do with him breaking up with me. Realistically, I know most relationships from high school don't last when you go to college, but I think what Justin and I had was different. Or, at least I thought it was. "Okay," I drawled out. "What exactly did he have to do with our break up?"

"Well, you already know he wasn't a big fan of us being together when we went off to college. He didn't exactly make that a secret. What you don't know is his reason for being that way."

"Which was?" I wish he would get on with it already. It'll help me decide whether to stay here and listen to what he has to say, or go find my cousin and act like the beginning of this evening never happened.

He gives me a sob story about how Justin and I reminded him of himself and Justin's mother. About how she ran off with somebody right before graduation and left his dad to care for the child. "His heart was in the right place, and at the time I thought it made sense."

He has got to be kidding me. That is probably the most ridiculous thing I've ever heard. "You're telling me that you dumped me because of your father's fears. After everything and all of our plans, that made sense to you? Justin, you are going to get your own apartment while we were still in high school just so we could be together and you would be out from under your dad's thumb. But you let that pull you away from me?"

"Audrey, I was 18 and terrified I would lose you to someone better off or smarter than I was. That's essentially what happened with my parents."

I cut him off. "And when did that fear actually come into place for you?" I get it, I do. At the same time, it makes absolutely no sense to me. "Was it before after your dad told you what happened with them?"

He staring at me with panic written all over his face. The answer to this question is going to determine how the rest of the night plays out. "Honestly, before." This is a surprise to me because he never let on that he questioned the relationship at all. Or, maybe that was just me viewing my love for him through rose colored glasses. "You were in all the honors classes, and busy with volunteer and after school activities. While I did good to make good grades while also working. We were already starting to spend less time together, and I felt like it wasn't going to work once we left high school. What if you joined a sorority or were too busy for me? I wasn't ready to set myself up for that kind of heartbreak after hearing what happened to dad."

This is all news to me. Even though we didn't see each other daily like we did before senior year, I always still went on dates frequently enough. "Instead, you made me go through it."

"If it makes you feel any better, I think it's probably one of the biggest mistakes I've ever made. Every time I would go home during school breaks, I would look for you while I was out running errands. I even drove by your house, but the lights were always off, and I was scared you would hate me." His voice trembles a little at that admission, and for a split second I feel awful for him.

"You would've been right," I say. Not to make him feel bad, but to let him know just how deeply he hurt me. "I changed all of my plans after you dumped me. It was hard enough going to school with you the last half of senior year, and I didn't think I could handle running into you while on campus."

"I'm so sorry, Audrey. If I could go back and do it all over again, there's so many things I would have changed. Not breaking up with you is one of them."

I believe him as crazy as it sounds. I've always had a knack for knowing when he's being sincere, and he is. And as much as it hurt then and hurt when I saw him again, I'm not sure I would have changed any of it. "Honestly, I think it turned out for the best." His shoulders sag and he's no longer looking at me. "It made me realize who I could be, and that I'm perfectly capable of standing on my own 2 feet despite what my cousins think."

"They always were pretty protective of you. And

judging how Tiffany yelled at me that night at the restaurant, they still are."

"Yeah, it's a little ridiculous, but they aren't so bad. At least I know they'll always be on my side." I take a drink, and gag. The drink would still be good if it wasn't watered down. As I push it toward the middle of the table and my hand brushes his.

"Well, that's all I came here to say. I think I should probably go now." He moves to stand and I place my hand on his arm.

"No, stay. While your reasoning doesn't make a lot of sense to me, I get it. I let the break up affect me way longer than I should have, and it took a long time for me to realize that." And if I'm being honest, I don't want him to go. It takes a lot of guts for someone to admit they were wrong, and he really isn't all that bad. Plus-side, I have somebody to sit at the table with me and I will be by myself while Tiffany and Spencer join the throng of people next to the stage.

"Are you sure?"

I nod, "As long as you get me something else to drink because I can't drink this. It's watered-down, and gross. Maybe a Margarita? They should have my name on a notepad up there, just tell them to put it on my tab."

"I got you." Well, I wish he would have said those words back then, I'm happy he's saying them now even if it's not the way I thought he would. And who knows, the night is still young.

Chapter Fourteen

Justin

I'm WAITING on the bartender to pour another drink for Audrey. The counter has people lined up, shoulder to shoulder. I don't think I've ever been to a bar to see a band play. Not that I've gone to many shows. I've been one hundred percent focused on my future and my job. I'm actually surprised Audrey comes to them. She was never one to go out like this when we were in high school. Tiffany was usually dragging her to parties she had no interest in attending. I'm almost certain it's the same thing here. This isn't her scene, or it wasn't. Things can definitely change in ten years.

The bartender slides the margarita toward me. "This is the most I've ever seen her drink." I don't tell him that she didn't actually drink the other two I got her. He might take offense about his bartending skills, and everything he's made is fine.

"Does she come here a lot?" I don't know why I ask. I

only want to know more about her, get a feel for the woman she is today.

He gives me a look like he doesn't know if he should say anything. Something must signal him in that I'm not horrible because eventually he does, "Only with Tiffany and Spencer. She doesn't usually come by herself."

"That's not surprising." I was right. And if I know Tiffany, she's doing it so Audrey won't spend too much time alone even though that's how she's always preferred to spend her nights. Cuddled up with a blanket and watching a movie.

"If any of you want anything else, just let me know. I'll be here all night." He grins at the woman standing next to me and grabs her drink order.

At least now I know she comes here often enough the bartender knows she doesn't drink much. She took my confession pretty well considering she also pretty much called me a coward. She has every right to think of me like that. I was a coward. I finally let my dad's words get into my head and boost the fears I had even more. I just can't believe she thought she meant nothing to me. She was my entire world, and if I play my cards right...she might be again.

I fight my way through the crowd until I see Audrey staring at her phone in disgust. After setting the drinks on the table, I try to spot Tiffany. It'll let me know if the look she's giving is because they are talking about me. But she has the same look on her face. So, not about me. "Did your phone do something to piss you off?"

"Look at this monstrosity." Audrey shoves the phone in my face. "Stella is nuts if she thinks I'm going to wear that. No single man will want to dance with me at her wedding if I'm wearing it." Well, that was a kick to the gut. I'm not sure when the wedding is, but I do know that she one hundred percent plans on being alone for it.

"It's not that bad," I smile, trying to play off the hurt. "I'd still dance with you. I'd dance with you if you were wearing a potato sack." It would also give me a chance to get her on a dance floor period. Because I'm a dumbass we didn't get that dance at senior prom. We didn't experience our lasts together the way we both assumed we would. Well, you know what they say about assumptions. Especially when the problem is one you created yourself.

"Yeah," she rolls her eyes. "Okay. This is worst that the dresses we picked out when we were drunk." That had to have been recently. Maybe she's changed more than I thought.

"Why were you drunk and picking out dresses? That sounds like a horrible idea."

Her cheeks blush in the dim light of the bar. Leaning back in her chair she puts her phone on the table and lifts her drink to her lips. "That's the night I ran into you."

Damn, she knows how to pack the punches. This is the third time she's had drinks in less than a week, by my count at least, and it's all because of me. Not only do I make her run away, but it seems I cause her to get drunk as well. The information is doing wonders for my self-esteem.

"Sorry I made you drink." I've never been the cause of someone's bad choices. "Was it really that bad seeing me?"

"Justin," she laughs. "I literally ran out in the middle of dinner. How did you think I was going to handle it? It sucked, for sure. But as long as we can be civil around each other then I don't see why we have to avoid each other." She takes another drink of her margarita waiting for me to respond. I have no clue how I'm going to do that without sounding like a dick.

"If it makes you feel any better, I really do wish I could go back and change everything." I would in a heartbeat. Even if things didn't turn out the way they have for each of us, I feel like I missed out on years we'll never be able to get back.

"Seriously, it's okay. I've had time to adjust to seeing you. It's not bad at all anymore. Luke told me I was being ridiculous." She bites her bottom lip again and I can't help wondering if she wants to try a relationship again. Though, I could have gone without her mentioning her coworker. Knowing that he's part of the reason she's back to feeling okay makes my blood boil. Too bad I don't deserve to have that feeling. Not when I was the cause.

"So, there's another reason I wanted to talk to you tonight. I have another question." I'm almost yelling to be heard over the music. "I was thinking, maybe we-"

I'm not able to finish the sentence. Audrey grabs my arm while setting her drink on the table and pulls me toward the crowd of people outside the roped off section. "Let's find Tiff and Spence." It's nowhere close to what I want to do, but she seems to need the distraction and I'll follow her anywhere. By the end of the night, I'm asking her for another chance whether she wants to hear it or not.

Audrey and I are leaning against a wall with Tiffany while Spencer does his thing at the merchandise booth with the band. His branding is the best I've seen, and I wonder why he doesn't try to get in contact with more bands.

"How did you like the show?" Audrey bumps into my

shoulder. For the first time since I've known her, she actually looks comfortable in a crowded space.

"They are actually really great. I was surprised."

"Why?" Tiffany scoffs. "They are amazing. And when they are playing on every radio station, I'm going to run around to everyone and tell them I told you so."

"This normally isn't my thing. That's all." I give Audrey a knowing look. This didn't used to be her thing either. "But I can see the appeal in coming to see them. It was the perfect way to blow off steam after a day at the office."

"That's the only reason Audrey comes," Tiffany points at her cousin. "I drag her out here knowing she'll have a good time before she does."

"You realize that if I *really* didn't want to come, I wouldn't, right? I like the band, and a night out every once in a while, isn't going to kill anyone." She argues. "Unless it's a work night. I typically bail on those. I like my sleep more than I like live music. Getting up early for work after a late night is the worst."

"So true," I agree. "The only morning person I know is Corinne, and she drives me crazy with her early breakfasts on the weekends. She also insists on making me a *balanced* meal before heading into the office. I love her, but I can't wait for her to go back home."

"I feel like I would get along great with your stepsister." Audrey beams.

"Who knows," I shrug. "Maybe that can be arranged before she drives me insane."

The crowd in the bar is thinning out as fans finish up their purchases. The band is signing items and Spencer takes that opportunity to come talk to us. "We should be done here in a few. We can take you home if you want, Audrey."

"I can take her." There's no way I'm letting anything else get in the way of me trying for another chance with her. "Her car is still at the office."

"Cuz?" Tiffany asks Audrey and lifts an eyebrow. She really is not a fan of me. I may have to win her approval first. It's the only way I can see any of this working without her being on my ass all the time.

"It's fine, Tiff." She reaches around me and gives her cousin a brief hug. "I'll call you the minute I get home."

"You better." Tiffany pulls out her phone and points to it. "Don't make me use our tracking system on you."

"You know good and well we haven't used that thing since you settled down." Audrey waves at her cousin and grabs me by the arm. "Let's get out of here before Tiff says anything else embarrassing."

She'll get no arguments from me.

Chapter Fifteen

Audrey

THE DRIVE back to the office is just like old times. Justin must have something on his mind. He has both hands on the steering wheel and leather squeaks the tiniest bit from here he's wringing it. The music on the radio is so quiet you can barely tell it's playing. It's an exact replay of how he acted when him and his dad got into arguments over a decade ago.

The urge to reach out and put my hand on his arm the way I did when we were teens is strong. Even after all this time it's second nature and I have to force myself to keep my hands in my lap. He glances over at me and I turn until all I can see are the brake lights in front of us.

This is weird and awkward. Like when you're on a first date with someone but you don't know what to say. The only difference is we have years of history behind us. As much as I want to, I'm not sure how to move past it. For now, I'm giving him the chance to gather whatever thoughts he has while I process what he told me at the bar.

I knew deep in my gut his dad had something to do with it. I just didn't think he'd stoop so low to create an emotional rift between me and Justin. The news that Justin had his own fears about us was new to me as well. I guess when you really love someone you look past all that, and clearly, he didn't love me enough. Not that I blame him. We *were* young. Neither of us knew anything about the big wide world we'd be stepping into. I wasn't lying when I told him it was probably for the best. That's something ten years of distance can give you...perspective. We may have ended up exactly where we are now. Or, we may have been so codependent on each other we would have held ourselves back and never flourished the way we were meant to.

Justin is still driving like he has a purpose, and I want to know what's in that skull of his. Tiffany was right when she said whatever he tells me could destroy me or make me want him. The conversation in the bar wasn't enough for either. Whatever he has to say when we get to the parking garage will be what does it. It'll be what gives me hope, or lets me know that there will never be anything between us again. Luke wasn't wrong when he said I still have feelings for him. In all honesty, they never went away. I wonder if that's true for all first loves or if it's singular to me because he was my world back then.

The silence is getting to me. I'm used to car rides listening to music as loud as I can stand it or the chattering of my cousins on speaker phone. Even at home I have something going so I don't feel quite so alone. One of us needs to break the silence before I get stuck in my head more than I already am. It's obvious he's not going to be the first one to do it. "Did you really like the show tonight?

Crooked Halo is quickly becoming one of my favorite bands."

"Yeah," His eyes never leave the road in front of him. Not one single glance my way. That shred of hope I had before, is withering away. "They were decent. Not what I usually listen to, but I can definitely see the appeal."

"They grow on you." I smile at the memory of Tiffany dragging me to one of their shows. I didn't think it was my speed either, but sometimes that grungy, rock is exactly what I need to get through the day. "If you stick around, you'll get to know the band. They are probably the most down to earth musicians I've ever met." Shit. I didn't mean to say that. Word vomit is the worst, and I practically threw out the words without thinking.

"Have you met a lot of musicians?" Now he looks at me, and from what I can tell, his eyebrow is raised a fraction. As if he can't believe *I* would ever be in that position to meet famous people. And why the hell can everyone I know do that eyebrow thing except me? From Stella it's disapproving and when Tiffany does it, you know she's about to wreak havoc on the world. Maybe I should practice more.

I shake the random thought away. "When Tiffany drags you to shows, and magically gets backstage and after the party passes, it's kind of hard not to."

"Wow." Is that...condescension coming from him? What was I supposed to do when I realized he wasn't coming back to confess his undying love for me? Sit around and be boring. I mean yeah, I'm pretty boring compared to my cousins, but seriously?

"Why is that so hard to believe?"

"I don't know," he shrugs, focusing on the road once again. The corner of his mouth tilts up the tiniest bit.

Maybe he isn't looking down on me. Ugh, it's so hard to read him now after all these years. "I just didn't think going to concerts was something you would be into. You've changed a lot since we were teens."

Could he give any more mixed messages? One minute he seems intrigued, the next it's like he misses the old me. The one that went along with every little thing and stayed in the shadows to stay away from attention. Not that much has changed. I *still* don't like the spotlight. But I do know how to go out and have a good time. It's not completely outside of my comfort zone any more. I've finally gotten to a point where I'm happy in my own skin. Sure, it's lonely because no other man has ever lived up to my idea of *him*, but the back and forth is getting old.

"It's not like I'm out there crowd surfing. I like live music. I just don't like the drunken idiots I usually encounter. It's also why I never go alone. I'm always with Tiffany and Spencer because they know my boundaries and back me up should an issue arise."

"Have there been any problems?"

"There was one time a guy wouldn't stop asking me out, but we handled it."

"How?" And now he's interested again. I'm getting whiplash.

"Tiffany threw his beer in his face. That ended things pretty fast. When I go, we don't go to the pit, we hang on the outskirts." Exactly where I like it.

"Now that I can totally picture," he laughs. "She really hasn't changed all that much since high school."

"No, she hasn't." She's fiery, passionate, and takes no shit. I admire her for all the qualities I don't possess. I should tell her that one day and let her know how much she means to me.

Finally, we pull up to the parking garage. He enters and parks next to my car. He takes his hands off the steering wheel and turns until he's facing me completely. The air is charged and it feels like possibility and heart-break. Maybe a mixture of the two. "It may not seem like it, but I did have fun tonight. It was nice seeing you let down your hair and live in the moment. It's all I've ever wanted for you. Even in high school."

"Thanks, I think?" There's no way to respond to that. "I had fun, too. It's nice to not be the third wheel. I always feel like I'm cramping their style and bow out of most outings."

"That's too bad. You look like you fit in. But I'll be around if you need someone with you." He slides his hand over the console, creeping closer to mine in my lap. Is he saying what I think he's saying? There's no way, right? He's been so wishy washy all night.

"What do you mean?" I need him to come right out and say it. No more of these stupid games. Luke tells me it makes the chase that much sweeter, but damn it. I don't want there to be a chase. I need to know point blank what his intentions are for me. What he wants out of whatever this weird thing is. The mental ping pong is getting old. I knew I'd forgive him and fall head over heels again the night Luke pointed out my feelings about Justin. Hopefully my heart doesn't suffer a repeat.

He scoots as close to me as he can while still in his own seat. "I mean, Audrey, I was an idiot at eighteen. Hell, I think most people are. But...I want to see if we can give this another go. To see where we might end up this time. Teenager me didn't know what he was doing. I let an irra-tional fear get in my head, and ruin what could have been the best thing for me. Would you consider dating me

again? To see if we're still as compatible as we used
to be."

My heart is beating double time in my chest. Everything I had hoped to hear so long ago just fell from his lips.
"What about work? Won't people talk?"

"Let them. It's not against the rules. I checked the
employee handbook." I don't bother telling him I know
that. Luke sent me an email with the page highlight in
bright yellow. I needed to know whether that would stop
him. It may be immature, but after he let his dad add to
the rift he was feeling, I want reassurance he won't let it
happen again.

I lean toward him until my lips are against his ear.
"Let's see where this goes."

He pulls back just enough for our eyes to meet.
Without a word, he thrusts his fingers into my hair and
slams his lips against mine. In so many ways it's just like
back then, but we're older and have experience we didn't
at eighteen. His tongue teases my lips open and I moan at
the contact. I'm not sure if it's because of him or the fact I
haven't been intimate in so long. Either way, I'm not
complaining.

When he breaks the kiss, both of us are panting. My
hair feels like it's all over the place and I rest my back
against the door. "I've wanted to do that since the day you
ran out of the elevator."

"Don't worry," I laugh. "You'll be able to do again."

"I hope so." He opens his door and comes around to
my side to open mine. "Will you come to dinner at my
place tomorrow?"

Stepping out of the car, I nod. "Sure. Want me to bring
anything?"

"Just yourself." He waits until I'm safely tucked away

in my car before he backs up to his own. "Goodnight, Audrey."

"Goodnight." The night could have ended a completely different way, and I'm so happy it looks like things are finally going my way in the relationship department.

Chapter Sixteen

Justin

NOTHING CAN BRING me down right now. I feel like that scene in Rocky where Stallone is standing on top of the stairs with his fists raised in victory. Asking Audrey to date me again was terrifying and this is one hundred percent that moment for me. It took me back to the very first time I asked her out. There weren't sweaty palms this time, but the nerves were probably worse. She could have shot me down and I wouldn't have blamed her. It's not like I've been a joy to be around.

The living room light is on as I walk up the sidewalk to the front door. Hopefully Corinne is asleep, and I won't have to deal with her and her million questions tonight. I open and close the door as quietly as I can. My feet are silent as I make my way across the rug.

"Are you whistling?" Corinne's head pops up over the couch. Fuck. I was so worried about a creaky floorboard and door that I forgot I was actually still making noise.

"So, what if I am?" I know I'm not ready for her interrogation. I'm tired and still have to figure out what exactly I'll attempt to cook for Audrey tomorrow night.

She doesn't say anything and I think I'm off the hook. I take a few more steps toward the hall. "I guess tonight went well?"

And...we're doing this. "Not that it's any of your business, but yes, it did."

"Good," she nods her head in approval. "When do I get to meet her?"

My dear, sweet, annoying sister has been bugging me to meet her since I mentioned working with her. Hell, she's been pushing me to ask Audrey out since she showed up in my kitchen. "Soon. She's coming over for dinner tomorrow night, but I need you to make yourself scarce."

"And miss my opportunity? Not a chance in hell."

"If you'd go back home, I wouldn't have to worry about having you leave." I feel like shit for even saying it. I'm the one person who has never judged her, and I'm being a dick right now because it's inconvenient for me. "Sorry, I didn't mean that. I do like having you here, but I want our second first date to be less of a community affair."

She shrugs away the hurt and that makes her a much better person than me. "I get it. I would be the same way. What am I supposed to do while you are occupied?"

"I'm sure there are more places you can photograph. Or, maybe you can hang out with Carter."

Her laugh is loud and echoes in the room. "I thought you didn't want me around him. Scared he's going to try to date me."

Maybe I should take Audrey out to eat instead. Corinne's right. I don't particularly want her around my best friend. Not because he isn't a good guy, he's just overly curious about her. And I don't want either of them to end up hurt if they dated. Not only will it suck seeing two of the most important people in my life in pain, but it puts me in the middle. I'd have to choose between family and friends. "You're right, I'll figure out something else."

"Don't be ridiculous. I'm perfectly capable of taking care of myself and pushing off any unwanted advances. This isn't the regency era. I have a voice." She stands and points her finger at me. "You need to have your date and catch up. There's a decade worth of learning to do between the two of you."

I laugh and take a step back. "I know you can handle yourself. It's him I'm worried about."

"Well, don't." She folds her arms across her chest. "What are you cooking for her? Do you need me to do anything?"

That's a great question because I still have no fucking clue. "Do you have any ideas on something easy?" She opens her mouth, but I cut her off. "I mean very easy. Something that even I can't screw up."

"Everything I know of is pretty boring. I could always cook before I head out."

It's a good idea. Her food is much more appetizing than whatever I would come up with. But no. I want the food to be prepared by me. And, if I can't come up with something, I'll order something and have it delivered before she gets here. "Boring is fine. I'm certain she's not expecting anything amazing. It's no secret that I lived off ramen and fast food our senior year of high school."

"Thank God you aren't trying to fix her ramen. That's definitely not going to wow her." She shakes her head, disgusted.

"Hey," I step back, hand on my chest in mock offense. "I found plenty of ways to jazz up some ramen. Don't knock it until you try it." I glance at the clock on the wall and my eyes widen. How the hell did it get so late? "I'm going to go to bed. It's been a long night. I'll make spaghetti or something. It's hard to screw that up, right?"

"It's relatively easy. I'll run to the store in the morning and get everything you need. Just leave your debit card on the counter."

Rolling my eyes, I pull my wallet out of my pocket. "Here," I grunt. "Can you bring back breakfast tacos, too?"

"Yep. Now get some sleep. We want you at your best tomorrow. You're gonna have to impress the hell out of her to keep her around forever."

What the fu—? Now, I'm nervous. I don't know that we'll end up as forever, but has she changed so much that I'll need to do some insane thing to keep her attention? I don't have the energy to worry about it. I walk down the hall toward my room. "Night, Sis." Nerves are a problem for tomorrow.

I feel like I need a checklist to make sure I have everything just right. I think Audrey might also like that idea. She's definitely way more organized than I've ever been. I did send her my address earlier, so at least that is out of the way, and now it's time for me to freak out even more. She should be here any minute.

The food is done and sitting inside the fancy bowls Corinne bought when she did the grocery run. Apparently, I can't just serve it out of the pans. I don't know why? All it's going to do is give me dishes to clean up after she leaves. I swear my sister is over the top extra and is doing more to make sure this date goes well than I am. There's just this fear that she's going to see all this work Corinne helped me do and realize that I'm a huge fake. That I'm not capable of this all the time.

Glancing at my phone, I check the time and see if I have any missed messages from Audrey. I'm good on that front, but I'm running out of the former. I grab the plates out of the cabinet and set them on the table, along with a bowl for the salad, and two forks. Should I put them next to each other with a plate on either side of the corner? Or, should I put them on either side of the table so we can be face to face over the food? Why the hell is this so hard? I place them in each spot at least five times before I decide on setting them next to each other. I don't want to be on the opposite side of the table from her.

Headlights coming down the road capture my attention from the kitchen window. Shit, shit, shit. That has to be her. I'm not ready. The last thing I need to do is light the candles. The car is driving slow and it will give me some time. I turn from the table and head toward the counter. Flinging the junk drawer open I rummage around for matches. A lighter. Something. I don't see them anywhere. I could have sworn I bought more the last time I did a run for emergency supplies. Apparently, I didn't.

The car that was creeping toward my house pulls into the driveway and the engine turns off. Time is up. I'll just brighten the lights a smidge and call it good. The candles can be decorative. I'm surprised Corinne didn't have the forethought to grab some when she was getting everything else. I'm almost terrified to look at my bank account. It will all be worth it if Audrey loves it, though.

I hear a car door close and pull some wine glasses from the hutch they are in and set them on the table. I rush back to the cabinets and pull down two glasses in case she'd rather have water. Going out to eat would have been so much easier than all of this.

As I set the glasses on the table, there's a knock on the door. Okay, Justin. You can do this. It's not like you're total strangers. Just be your normal charming self. That might be part of the problem. With a deep breath, I make my way to the front door. One more breath as I put my hand on the door knob and turn. Please let her like this.

I don't think I've ever been this insecure about a damn date. Time to see if it pays off. I pull the door open and my mouth drops open.

Chapter Seventeen

Audrey

WHY IS he looking at me like that? Do I have something on me? I take a moment to glance over my outfit. I don't see any stains. Surely Tiff would have said something if there was something wrong with the dress. Despite her feelings about Justin, she came over and helped me get ready. She even brought some of her clothes for me to wear, but I'm a bit bustier than her. I also wouldn't have felt comfortable in clothes that weren't mine. I'm trying to do everything in my power to make sure this date goes well.

When I look up, he's still wide-eyed with his mouth hanging open. I shift on my feet. "Is, um, everything okay?" Geez, that didn't come out strong and confident at all. I sound like a girl who's unsure of herself and needs approval. Probably because I am. Dating isn't new territory for me, but dating an ex who broke up with me…that is one hundred percent new.

His mouth snaps closed and he shakes his head. "Not

at all." Opening the door wider, he motions me inside. "You look amazing."

That's a relief. Tiffany found this black dress in the back of my closet. I don't even remember the last time I wore it. Honestly, I didn't even think it would still fit. It's low cut and shows just enough cleavage to tease, but not so much that I'm falling out of it. And it stops mid-thigh with a skater skirt. It's cute, comfortable, and I feel amazing in it. I swear my cousins know me better than myself sometimes when it comes to my clothes. "Thank you."

He waits for me to walk through the door and closes it behind me. "You can set your bag here or in the living room." He points toward the entryway table and I slide my small purse off my shoulder and set it down. "The kitchen, and more importantly dinner, is right through here."

He walks closer to me as he leads me to the kitchen. His hand so close it brushes mine. As immature as it might seem, butterflies erupt in my stomach at the small contact. A part of me wishes he would grab my hand already and pull me toward him. Maybe it's been too long since I've been touched by a man, or the fact that it's him, but after our kiss last night, all I can think about is his hands all over me. Focus, Audrey. You have to see what's even going to happen before you try ending up in bed with him.

The kitchen is dimly lit and pretty bowls are lined up in the middle of the table. It's not so dark that you can't see, but it helps the mood for the night. At least I'm not the only one trying to set the tone for the evening.

"Did you cook all this?" I lean over the table and see

pasta, sauce and meatballs in each of the dishes. A gigantic salad sits in a bowl to the side. When did he learn how to cook? He was never that great at it when we were in high school and burnt more than food than I can recall. "It smells amazing."

"Thanks." His cheeks redden and I find it funny that I'm the one causing him to blush. It's always been the other way around. "Corinne left me very detailed instructions on how to not fuck it up."

I almost forgot his step-sister has been here. "Where is she anyway? Did she go back home?" I want to meet her. Not only because he obviously cares for her like they've been siblings all their lives, but also so I can try to pry stories out of her. She's known him for the time I've been away from him. It'll give me a deeper look into who he is now from another perspective.

"No, she's still here." At my expression he waves his hands in the air. "Not like right now. She went to hang out with Carter and take pictures or something. She's out of our hair for the night so we can have a proper date without her asking you a million questions."

So, she knows Carter. I guess he's been friends with him for a long time if his sister feels comfortable going out on the town. "Are they together?"

"They better never be," Justin growls and I can't stop the laugh that bubbles out of me. There's the protective man I know. "What's so funny?"

"Nothing." I'm still giggling and do my best to rein it in. "It's just been so long since I've seen you like this. I remember you'd get that way when some jockhole we went to school with would pick on me."

"Well," he throws his arm over my shoulder and I

relish the touch. He pulls me closer to him. "Nobody messes with my girl." For a whole two seconds I think he's going to bend down and meld his lips to mine, but he clears his throat and points to the chairs with plates in front of them. "Are you ready to eat?"

He has to be just as nervous as I am. He's never gone through this much work to impress me. Don't get me wrong, he set up an amazing backyard picnic with the help of my cousins the summer before senior year, but nothing like this for a run of the mill date. I take a seat and wait until he's sitting before asking, "What happened to Corinne to make you so protective?"

"She hasn't exactly had the best track record with dating. Most guys treat her like shit or they use her until she doesn't have anything else to offer before they split. It's only ever been her and her mom until me and Dad. It felt right to do what I could to help be a big brother even though she's slightly older than me." He points at the table, "Let's eat before the food gets cold."

It's good to know that even after all this time nothing has really changed with him. He's still down to earth from what I can see and takes care of those he feels are impor-tant to him. Sitting here with him now feels like it's been forever and also like no time has passed since we were those lovestruck teenagers.

I pile my plate with food, take a bite, and moan. "This is really good. It may even be better than most Italian restaurants."

"Yeah," he croaks. "I'm going to need you to stop making that sound."

"Well, you shouldn't cook really good food. I can't help how my body reacts." Now that the words are out of my mouth, I can't help agonizing over them. Did it sound bitchy? I was going for flirting, but I've never been great at it. It's one of the things I wished my cousins would teach me because they are pros. I'm awkward to put it mildly.

Justin mumbles something under his breath before shoving a forkful of spaghetti into his mouth.

"What was that?" All I heard was something about showing me how my body reacts.

He sets his fork on the plate and pins me with a stare. He looks like he'd rather have me for dinner. "I said, I can help show your body how to react." His voice is much deeper than it was even seconds before and his jaw is tight.

Be flirty, Audrey. It's not that hard. "Wine me, dine me, and then maybe you can show me."

The rest of dinner was very anticlimactic. We talked about what we've been doing the past ten years. Me working in my cubicle, minding my own business, and him working his way up the ladder at the accounting firm that's now merged with ours. Basically, we're both boring. Though, I think I've lived it up a little more than he has thanks to Tiffany. She drags me to shows any chance she gets and any time I say yes.

I rinse off my plate and put it in the dishwasher despite his protests. It's ingrained in me. Mom always made us clean up after ourselves when we were kids. He knows that, and I don't know why he's acting surprised. I don't realize he's standing right behind me until he asks, "Do you have room for dessert?"

"What kind?" That's the important question. Does it

mean actual food? Or, me and him having each other? This new highly sexual Audrey is a shock. I feel like Tiffany would be proud of me for putting myself out there. For hinting at what I want. Justin is the only person I can think of that I'm remotely comfortable being like this around. Even though we've only just reconnected, I've known him my entire life. He was all of my firsts. He's the only one that can pull out this side of me.

"That depends," he leans on the counter next me and winks, "I have tiramisu in the fridge, but if you have other things in mind, I wouldn't mind."

"Well, when you put it like that…" I turn toward the fridge and open the door. There is a massive pan with what I can only imagine holds the delicious coffee cake. I pull it out of the fridge and set it on the counter. "Did you make this too?"

He snorts, "Please, I could barely pull off the spaghetti. I do not have the talent to make a cake like that."

Instead of looking for a plate, I search the drawers until I find a fork. I dip it into the cake and pull out a forkful, lifting it to Justin's mouth, waiting for him to take the bite. He doesn't disappoint. The way his mouth moves over the fork is slow and seductive. Who knew eating could be such a turn on? "Is it good?"

He nods and pulls the fork from my hand. "See for yourself." He scoops some out and feeds me in the same exact way. I try to do what he did but I feel like a moron.

Another moan escapes my lips as I close my eyes and savor the moment. The way I feel with him feeding me, and how delicious the cake is. "Can I take some of that home with me?"

"You can have whatever you want." A tiny smirk lifts up the corner of his mouth. "You've got something right

—." He doesn't finish the sentence. Leaning in he lifts his hand as if to wipe away whatever piece of cake is on my face, but at the last second, he drops it around my waist and pulls me flush to him. His lips are on my mouth in seconds, and I know right now all bets are off. The likelihood of me going home tonight is zero.

Chapter Eighteen

Justin

AUDREY MOANS into my mouth at the contact. She has to
know I did it on purpose. I didn't even try to play it off too
much. The icing on her mouth? Total cliche, but it was
worth it. I purposefully slid the fork into her mouth at an
angle. I wanted an excuse to get my lips on hers. Ever
since she made that damn comment during dinner, it's all
I've ever been able to think about.

She throws her arms around my neck and deepens the
kiss. This woman manages to steal my heart over and over
again. It doesn't seem to matter what age we are. Now, it's
my turn to groan. Her lips are soft and full. I move to kiss
her cheek then her neck. She's so damn short that I have to
bend over. Without warning, I pick her up to sit on the
counter. She spreads her legs wide enough for me to nestle
between them. Her breathing is ragged as I continue
kissing her skin.

Dragging my lips up her neck once again, I stop when I
get to her ear. Nibbling her lobe until her legs wrap

around my waist and she pulls me closer to her. "Please, don't stop."

"I don't plan on it." I pause for a second before I continue worshipping her skin.

She leans back, resting her weight on her hands, giving me access to the rest of her body. She's definitely more open now than she was back then, and I'm not complaining one bit. My lips follow the line of her shirt and the cleavage on full display. Trailing my fingers from her waist to her breast, I softly squeeze until she's moaning again. "Justin, I need you to—."

"Need me to what?" I hope like hell she was going to finish that with fuck me, but I don't know that she'd ever say that in a million years.

"I don't know," she pants. "Something."

Instead of replying, I slide my hand down her breast with just enough pressure to cause friction. We both may be fully clothed, but it doesn't matter. My hand follows the path down her stomach before lifting her skirt and rubbing along her inner thigh. "Tell me what you want."

Her breath hitches. "I want you to make me feel good."

"That I can do." I press my lips to hers as I let my finger slip beneath her panties into her wet pussy. Jesus, she feels good. My tongue dances with hers, and I rub her clit with my thumb. She takes the weight off one arm and grabs my shirt, yanking me closer. She shifts her hips until she's grinding my hand, and fuck, I'm going to come before I'm ready.

She's buzzing with pent up energy, and I want to taste her before she comes undone. Breaking the kiss, I feverishly kiss down her body as I pull her panties down and get on my knees before her. "You deserve to be fucking worshipped." I don't wait for a response. My lips meet her sweet folds and I groan. "You taste so good," I mumble against her.

Her fingers are in my hair and she's pulling me closer. Riding my mouth to get closer to that sweet release. My tongue swirls around her clit and her legs shake. "I'm so close, Justin."

I slide a finger into her and pump until her body goes tight and she's all but screaming my name. That won't be the last time my name falls from her lips in pleasure tonight.

"What the hell? Tell me you're not doing what I think you are on the counter where I prepare food." Oh shit. No, no, no. What the fuck is she doing here?

"Get out, Corinne," I bark.

"Oh my God." Audrey pulls away from me and jumps down from the counter. I barely stop myself from falling backward at the force of her landing. "This is so embarrassing." She pulls her panties up and her face is bright red. "I think I should go."

"No," I reach out to grab her hand. "Don't. I'll find out why she's back already. You can go hang out in my room if you don't want to stay out here." She starts to argue, but I pull her down to my level. "It's not the end of the world, I promise. I'll smooth things over with my sister. I want you to stay."

She bites her lip and glances toward the entryway. I can see the indecision warring in her eyes. Finally, she sighs, "Okay, I'll stay. Which way is your room? I'm not leaving this spot until you have your sister distracted."

"Thank you," I whisper and give her a quick peck on the cheek. "Give me a couple of seconds. Just follow the hallway. My room is the one at the end of it. If you look through my drawers, I should have some t-shirts and sweats you can wear."

She snorts. "Who said I was staying the night?"

At least I can make her laugh past her mortification. "Um, me. Besides we have plans then I intend to order breakfast to be delivered. How do you feel about breakfast tacos?"

She rolls her eyes and shoos me away. "We'll talk about that later."

"Fine." I stand up and smile down at her. "I'm glad you're here." Before going to the living room, I make a quick stop at the table, grab a napkin, and wipe my face. I plan on doing more of that later.

Corinne is standing by the front window when I walk in. "Why are you already back? You weren't supposed to come home until a lot later than now." My voice is strained and I'm trying to keep my cool. She did me a huge favor by leaving for a majority of the night, but she could have called.

"I'm sorry, Little Brother." She put emphasis on the little. "I forgot my extra battery and Carter stopped by here so we could grab it before going downtown. I thought y'all would still be eating dinner, or watching a movie. I didn't expect to walk into, well, that. How was I supposed to know y'all would be getting down and dirty on the kitchen counter?" She crosses her arms and glares at me. "You're going to sanitize the counter, right? I love you, but I don't know if I can cook in the kitchen again until I know it's clean."

"You are impossible." I rub my hand over my face. "Of course, I'm going to clean. I'm not an idiot." I take a few seconds to think about what she just said. "Wait. Carter is in the driveaway?"

"Yeah," she shrugs. "I was supposed to be in and out, not scarred for the rest of my life. I don't think I'll ever unsee that."

"You better not utter a word to him." She likes to talk, and I have a feeling, despite my warning he's going to find out anyway. "I mean it, Rinne. He'll give me hell for days."

"I won't tell him. Do you honestly think I want to relive that?" I'm hoping by keeping her attention on me, Audrey has already slipped off to my room. "But I expect to properly meet her soon."

"You will after she's gotten over her embarrassment." She'll most likely meet her in the morning. "Are you coming home tonight?"

"Duh," she spits out. "I like Carter and all, but I'm not staying at his place. Have you seen it? It's messier than anything I've ever encountered. That includes the deadbeats I've dated."

"Well, that's good to know." Honestly, I think she protests too much and too quickly. "I guess I'll see you in the morning, then." I don't wait for a response. I need to make sure Audrey has calmed down. She's most likely freaking out that she's made a bad first impression.

When I open the door, Audrey is sitting on the edge of my bed wearing one of my old t-shirts. It's reminiscent of when she used to wear my hoodies to school. It's like a status saying she's mine, and I'm happy she had no qualms about putting it on. "Are you okay?"

She turns and looks at me, her long brown curls hanging over her shoulder. "Is your sister gone?"

"She will be soon. Apparently, she forgot to take her extra camera battery. She won't be back until later tonight." I sit next to her and wrap an arm around her waist, pulling her toward me.

She leans her head on my shoulder. "That wasn't how I planned on meeting her you know? Hopefully she doesn't think I'm an awful person."

I laugh and kiss the top of her head. "She doesn't. She was just taken off guard. Besides, she doesn't get the right to judge you, or me. This is my house."

"Yeah," she sighs. "But she's a guest and you should have some sort of respect for that."

"Eh, I do. But the same goes for her. She tends to have boundary issues and needs to know everything. It's kind of annoying."

"Most siblings are from what I've seen." She leans back. "Though, I guess I have some experience since my cousins are almost like my siblings." She laughs for a second. "Can you imagine the trouble any of our parents would have had if we were sisters and lived under the same roof all the time? We would have driven them crazy."

"That's no lie. The three of you together are a handful. But I was always a little jealous of the bond you had. I never had that close of a relationship with anyone outside of y'all. Now that I have it, I totally get why your bond was so strong." I lean back until I'm lying on the bed, dragging Audrey back with me. "Having that means a lot, and we have each other's back when shit goes down. Which is why she's here. And it's also why she has no room for judgement. She's made plenty of bad decisions."

"Are you saying that was a bad choice?" Audrey smiles up at me. "Because from where I'm standing, it was the best one I've made in a really long time."

"There was no mistake in what happened in the kitchen," I wink at her. "Maybe we should continue where we left off."

I'm waggling my eyebrows at her and she snorts before hitting lightly on the chest. "Maybe later, I'm still pretty mortified. Hell, I don't even know how I'm going to look her in the eye without thinking about how she saw us."

"Well, what do you want to do?"

She taps her chin, deep in thought. "Let's watch a movie. You have popcorn, right?"

"Yes, but it's not going to be one of those cheesy romances you used to make me watch when we were in school is it? I don't know if I have the mental energy to watch that."

"Fine," she sighs. "You can pick the movie, but just know there's a possibility I'll pass out during an action movie."

"Chick flick it is." I pull both of us up and peek out of the door to make sure Corinne is really gone. If I play my cards right, I'll have Audrey in my bed before the movie is even over.

Chapter Nineteen

Audrey

THE HOUSE IS quiet when I wake up. Justin is lying next to me, shirtless, and I want more than anything to run my fingers along his chest. Wake him up and spend hours making love to each other the way we did last night. He's a lot more experienced now, and I have a feeling we've barely tapped the surface of what we can make each other feel.

I need to get out of here, though. Not because of anything he did, but because I don't want to run into Corinne. That will be an awkward conversation and I'm not ready to have it. Hopefully, Justin isn't to upset with me when he wakes up.

I slide out of the covers and bed, and when my feet meet the floor, I check behind me to see if he's stirred. All I can hear is light snoring coming from his side of the bed. The sweats he found for me are on the floor and I move to put them on. The thought to change and put my dress back on enters my mind, but I brush it off just as quickly. It will only add time to my departure and I'm trying to creep out of here like a thief in the night. How the hell did Tiffany do this all the time before she met Spencer? It feels so cruel to leave someone in bed while you scamper off.

The bedroom door is open a fraction and I pull it wider, listening for any creak or noise that might give me away. That would look way worse than him waking up to me gone. Catching me leaving…I think that would be a slap in the face.

Tiptoeing down the hall, I'm at the entryway table bag and keys in hand when his voice stops me in my tracks. "Going somewhere?"

Damn it. Busted. There are two ways to play this cute and dumb, or give him the truth. The only problem is he'll see straight through the former. Guess honesty wins. Not that I'm upset about it, I just don't know if I'm ready for meet the family. I've had issues with his Dad, and the thought of meeting his sister has me going back to eighteen-year old me when I was doing my best to get his dad to love me. Hell, I would have been grateful if he even liked me. "I was, uh, going to go home."

"This early?" He raises an eyebrow in question.

"I have things to do before work tomorrow?" Ugh, that was pathetic. Who the hell answers with a question?

"You can stop bullshitting me, Audrey. I know you have your laundry done well in advance, and your place is probably spotless." Well, shit. He has me all figured out. He crosses his arms and his muscles flex. I know exactly what he can do with his arms. And if I'm being honest with myself, I want to be wrapped up in them.

"I just…doesn't this seem really fast? Last night was our first date and I've already ended up in your bed. Then there's the pressure of meeting Corinne, and I'm not sure I can handle that." My eyes roam the room, looking anywhere but at him. Anything to keep my focus off him. To keep me from jumping in his arms without a moment's notice. "I mean you saw how well received I've been by family members before."

"First of all, Corinne isn't like that. You'll love each other." He takes slow, cautious steps toward me, as if I'll skitter away. "And believe it or not, my dad has changed quite a bit. There's no reason for you to go home. Not yet."

Luckily, I don't have to see his dad anytime soon. All that excitement I had about meeting his sister is waning after what she walked in on last night. I don't understand how he's so cool with it. The way he acts as if it wasn't a big deal. Or, maybe it is, and he's doing everything he can to keep me calm. "Promise she won't make it weird." That's ridiculous though. I'm more likely to make it awkward as hell. These are the times I wish I was more like Tiffany. She would have laughed the incident off and gone about her day. Me? No, I have to sit there and dwell on it. I stopped thinking about it last night because out of sight, out of mind and all that. But this morning is a different story. She's in one of the bedrooms off the hallway.

"She won't." He finally reaches me and grabs my hand. "Come back to bed and in a couple of hours I'll order breakfast. After that, if you're still feeling skittish, I'll tell Corinne that you'll meet her some other time. Deal?"

I'm not good with making decisions for myself. When anyone else comes to me with a problem, I can think of a million solutions. At this moment, I'm having a hard time deciding. If I leave, Justin will be disappointed. If I don't, I'm opening myself up to be hurt by yet another one of his family members. I'm about to say no. It's on the tip of my tongue, but I can't. I promised this man I'd give us a fresh start. I can't do that if I'm holding on to the fear of his family not liking me. It's time to put my big girl panties on and give this thing an actual chance. "Deal."

I allow him to lead me back to his room. "So, you were just going to take off in my clothes? What if those were my favorite ones?"

"You would have been out of luck." I grin up at him. And just like that we fall right back into teasing banter. He's always been the one that can calm me down, and he hasn't lost the touch.

We enter his room and he closes then locks the door behind us. Within seconds we're in his bed and he's pulling my shirt off. I can do this. I can be with him and not worry about my likability.

What feels like half a day later, but in reality, it's only a couple of hours, Justin leans on his elbow and stares down at me. "Are you ready to meet Rinne? Or, do you want to duck out? Before you overthink yourself to death, just know that I'm fine with either decision."

Of course, he is. He'll always do whatever he can to ease my fears and make sure I'm comfortable. Even if that means not doing the one thing, he wants me to. It's one of the reasons I love him. Wait. Loved. It's one of the reasons I *loved* him. We may have past ties, but there's no way I can just pick up where we left off. Not completely. We're both drastically different than we were all those years ago.

"Audrey?" He tilts his head like a confused puppy and I can't help smiling. Oh yeah, he asked a question.

"Sure. I mean as nervous as I am, I should probably go

ahead and get it over with." That is definitely the best option. It's better to find out if she'll hate me now rather than later. I have to protect my own mental health.

"Well, let's do this then." He climbs out of bed and puts his clothes on. I watch every muscle in his arm as he lifts the shirt over his head and pulls it down. "Just put my shirts and sweats back on. I'm not even sure where you put your dress."

"It's folded on the dresser," I say.

He waits for me to get dressed and holds his hand out for mine. "You ready?"

I nod. It's the only answer I can give. I don't know if I'm ready or not, but there isn't much choice now.

His sister is in the kitchen making breakfast tacos. "I thought you were going to have some delivered?"

He rolls his eyes and nods toward her. "I was, but Corinne over here is an overachiever and thinks I should eat less fast food. She prefers to cook breakfast while she's here."

"And lunch and dinner," she sing songs.

"Those too." He pulls me closer to the stove. "Corinne, this is Audrey. Audrey, my pain in the ass sister, Corinne."

"It's nice to meet you," she beams at me.

"You too." Good she's not going to say anything about last night. Everything might end up okay. "How long are you in town?"

"Until my ex-boyfriend gets his shit out of my place." She pushes the scrambled eggs around the pan. "I may have to get a few friends involved. I never intended to stay this long, and I'm eventually going to have to get back to work. I have appointments coming up."

"What do you do?" I know Justin mentioned she forgot her camera battery, but I don't want to assume anything.

"I'm a photographer. Mostly family portraits, but a few weddings here and there." She shrugs her shoulders as if it's no big deal.

"That's amazing." I want to take a look at her work. "My cousin is actually getting married in the Fall. Maybe I can hook you two up."

"That would be awesome," she smiles. "I'll get you one of my cards to give her. I'll go pretty much anywhere. I'm always up for an adventure."

Justin gives me a huge grin that says I told you so. "Now that girl bonding time is over, is breakfast almost ready? I'm starving."

"I'm sure," Corinne rolls her eyes. "Go set the table. I only need to heat up the tortillas."

"Aye, aye, Captain." He pulls me toward the table. "You sit. I've got this."

I watch the two of them interact and it's like watching me with my cousins. Justin was right. There was no reason for me to worry. I can already tell I'm going to get along with Corinne fabulously.

Chapter Twenty

Justin

AUDREY IS STEPPING onto the elevator, and I rush behind her and grab her around the waist. "I've missed you so much."

She's been busy helping Stella get things ready for the wedding. While I'm happy for Stella, I'm not so happy that my time with Audrey is being cut short. I'm just happy they finally decided on a dress, and Audrey can stop complaining about the horrible choices Stella sends her.

"I thought we said no PDA while at work," Audrey screeches. The fact that she's leaning into me and smiling tells me she's not all that mad. "People are going to start talking."

I place a quick peck on her neck and whisper in her ear, "People are already talking." I mean, she couldn't expect it to stay quiet. Not when one of her best friends is Luke and he has a habit of saying anything that enters his mind. Although, all those questions he was asking me before Audrey agreed to date me all over again are beginning to make sense now. He was her scout, and he was digging for information. If I was half as smart as he is, I would have had Carter doing my dirty work for me. Except, Carter already knew somehow, and I was too stupid to realize it.

"No, they're not." She slaps my shoulder and then stands on her tiptoes to kiss me. "They are probably just wondering why I'm in such a good mood."

"I don't think you were ever in a bad mood before the merge, but definitely think they can tell something is up. Especially with how often you come to my office, and how many times we go to lunch together." The elevator doors open, and another person gets on. "Besides," I whisper. "You're acting like they can't think for themselves, and we haven't exactly been discrete."

Her only response is a shrug. She knows she's being naïve about our coworkers, but I'll go with it. She can live in the fantasy world as long as she wants.

"So, are you coming to dinner with me, Tiffany, and Spencer?" Her eyes are wide and she reminds me of a sad puppy. There's absolutely zero way I can say no to that. Even if Tiffany scares the hell out of me. She's not quite as forgiving as Audrey, and she makes a point of letting me exactly how much she dislikes me any time I see her. And Spencer, intelligent man that he is, doesn't interfere. I feel like he sympathizes with me, though.

"I could have sworn I already told you I was. Besides, I'm planning on riding with you because Corinne has my car."

"Why?" The door opens again on our floor, and both of us step out of the same time.

"Her car is making some kind of noise, and she's freaking out. Instead of getting a new car, she's throwing an insane amount of money at this one. With as much driving as she does, she'd be better off getting another one and writing it off on her taxes." I already know how Audrey is going to argue this point. She will be firmly on Corinne's side. Hell, the car she's driving is at least a decade old, but she refuses to upgrade because it's still perfectly drivable.

"You know, you have to let her make her own decisions. As someone who is constantly being pushed around by my oldest and youngest cousin, I get where she's coming from. She'll figure out what's best for her, or be stuck on the side of the road needing you to come rescue her." She glances up at me. "When is she going home anyway? There's no way her ex is still slumming it at her place. Hasn't it been like two months?"

I've been asking myself the same thing. Not that I don't love her, but she's starting to get on my nerves. Whenever Audrey and I want to hang out, we usually have to go to her place because Corinne invites herself to stay and hang out with us. How can you properly date someone when you're never alone? "It has. I plan on asking her about it soon. Honestly I think she's starting to love it here."

"It's hard not to. Even with a city this size there are so many things to do. I don't think I've uncovered half of Austin's secrets and I've been here for what feels like forever." As much as she doesn't care for being in crowds, she has a wanderer's heart. She likes to explore and see what she can find no matter where she is.

"True, but it'd be nice if she fell in love and explored from her own place, not mine."

"Yeah, it does put a damper on things sometimes and my place isn't very big. The walls are also really thin." She winks at me before stepping away. "See you at lunch?"

"Absolutely." She heads to her cubicle and I go to my

office. It's almost the end of the month…again. The one time that we're all insanely busy. Some of us even work longer hours just to make sure everything gets closed out.

I'm booting up my computer and getting my desk ready for the day when Carter walks in. He pulls one of the chairs right next to my desk and plops into it. "So, it looks like your love life is panning out pretty well."

"I guess," I shrug and continue signing into my computer. "It's only been a month since we started dating. She doesn't want to rush things and I'm respecting that boundary."

"Dude, y'all are all over each other. Don't think the rest of us haven't noticed the frequent trips to the copy room." He grins and slaps his hand on the desk. "I'm pretty sure y'all are it for each other."

"There's no pretty sure. I knew at sixteen she was it for me. I just had an idiotic streak when I was eighteen."

"At least you're correcting it now. That's better than nothing, and she seems to be on board. At least from where I'm sitting." Here he is stating the obvious once again. As if I need help seeing what's right in front of me.

"What have you been up to? I haven't seen you in a bit." There are already twenty emails needing my attention, and I know it's going to be a long day.

"Well, you've been preoccupied with a certain brunette," he laughs. "But not much. Trying to figure out why Corinne is dodging me. She asked if I could show her some spots to take photos and then bailed on me."

"Man, I don't know. She's been acting off, but she's probably figuring out her stuff for work. I think she has actual appointments coming up." I click the first message and make notes of everything that needs to be done before I respond. "I can ask her if you want."

"It's all good. What are you doing this weekend?" He glances around to see if anyone needs him. "Want to grab drinks? It's been a while."

"Sure. I think Audrey is visiting Stella so they can see the dress she wants in person." He's being weird. Well, weirder than normal.

He stands and pushes the chair back to where it was. "Cool. I'll get out of your hair. I need to check on a few reports. I swear if I see one more worksheet I'm going to scream. I'm just ready for the weekend."

"Me too. Let me know if you need any help with the worksheets." I see his outline leave the room and I dig into my work. It's going to be a long, busy day. Sadly, I think my lunch date is going to have to be postponed.

"Shouldn't you be getting ready?" Audrey throws one of my shirts at me. I've already started leaving clothes here for moments just like this. As much as I can pull off a suit, I don't want to wear it after work hours. It gives off a stuffy vibe.

"Probably," I shrug. "It's kind of hard when you're walking around the apartment half naked."

"That's because I'm actually getting ready." She steps into her closet and slides hangers to the right. I don't even know what she's looking for. It's not like it's a formal dinner or anything. We're meeting at the diner where Tiffany works.

I don't even understand how Spencer and I got roped into going. We literally have zero purpose for being there. They are planning Stella's bachelorette party and I'm certain I don't want any of those details. I only hope it doesn't involve a strip club. Just the idea of some random dude grinding on my girl has me wanting to fight.

Instead of arguing with her, I walk slowly to her and put my arms around her waist. "You act like we have to be there at a certain time. You know your cousin is always late."

"That doesn't mean we have to be." Her words are breathy. That could be because I'm sliding my hand over her stomach and continuing on south. Before I have a chance to slip my hand beneath her panties, she spins away from me. "Oh, no. You aren't distracting me this time."

"I don't know what you're talking about." Damn, I was really hoping that was going to work.

"You know exactly what I'm talking about." She jabs her finger into my chest. "You are not allowed to use your magical fingers, or tongue, until we get back. Tiffany and I have a lot to get planned. Stella's wedding is creeping up on us, and we're not prepared for anything, except the photographer, food and DJ."

"Fine," I pout. "Though you know most of the night will be spent with Tiffany glaring at me, right? Is she ever going to like me and welcome me back into the circle again?"

"I don't know," She tosses the words over her shoulder as she pulls out a dress. It has flowers and a low-cut top. She's trying to fucking kill me, I swear. "You know how she is. Holding grudges will always be something she does until she sees a reason to let it go."

"Yeah, but that was over a decade ago. Who the hell holds a decade long grudge?" It's infuriating.

"It's like you've never met my cousin. She still doesn't like some of her classmates from kindergarten." She thinks for a moment before slipping the dress over her head. "Actually, she ignores one kid completely, even now. All because he left her outside during one of mom's Halloween parties, and that was well over twenty years ago. Never underestimate my cousin's temper."

That's way too long to dislike someone over something so trivial. I'm sure the other kid doesn't even remember. "Fine. I'll play nice, but don't think I won't grill Spencer on what I can do to make her at least tolerate me."

"Good luck," she giggles. "She's got that man wrapped around her finger."

"Huh," I grunt. "Sounds familiar."

"Oh please, if anything it's you always wanting time together. I don't even remember the last time I slept alone." Wow, way to make a man feel wanted. She sees my expression as she turns, modeling the dress. "I didn't mean it like that. We're almost seamlessly falling into our old patterns. What if we lose ourselves in the process?"

This sounds like second thoughts about us, and I don't like it. "If it makes you feel any better, I actually have plans with Carter while you're with your cousins."

She nods. "Good. We didn't have any friends outside of us back then. I don't want that to happen again."

"Me either." I think back to how my dad described his relationship with Mom, and I can't help but wonder if Audrey and I are bound to the same fate. Minus the college classes, of course. Speaking of, I have a question I've never asked her. "Why didn't you go to Hilltown like you planned?" It's something that always bothered me.

That stops her in her tracks. Maybe I shouldn't have said anything. "I couldn't," she pauses. "Not with you there. We were on the same course track. Running into you would have been inevitable, and at the time my heart couldn't bear it."

Damn it. That's exactly what I didn't want to hear. "I feel like I robbed you of your college experience. I hope you know that was never my intention."

"I know." She closes the distance between us. "I didn't get it at the time, and it took a while. But I ended up okay." When I begin to speak, she places a finger over my mouth. "We ended up okay. We're never going to be able to move forward if we dwell on the past."

I tip her chin up until her mouth is aligned with mine. I know she won't let me kiss her senseless, so I settle for brushing my lips over hers one, two, three times. "You're right. Are you almost ready?"

"Yep. I just need to grab my bag and we can head out." She places her lips to mine once again. "I'll talk to Tiffany. Even if she doesn't understand, she can at least be nice."

I've never been so happy that she isn't like her younger cousin. Hell, if she was, she never would have given me, us, a second chance.

Chapter Twenty-One

Audrey

WE PRETTY MUCH HAVE THE diner to ourselves, so we can be
as loud as we want. Because I have a feeling, they will be
some screaming matches between me and Tiffany tonight.
There's a good chance she's not going to agree with some
of the things I think we should do for the bachelorette
party, and she's going to want to go all out, but I know
Stella better than that. She likes to go out, but this is the
night about her, not what Tiffany wants to drag us around
town doing.

"Do you want anything else to drink?" Justin leans over
and whispers in my ear. He's sitting as far away from
Tiffany as he can. I don't blame him. She's done nothing
but shoot him icy glares since we came in.

"No, I'm good." I tap Tiffany on the arm to get her
attention. "Come with me to the ladies room?"

She scoffs, "I am pretty sure you're perfectly capable of
going to the restroom by yourself."

"Now, Tiffany." She is going to have to get used to

Justin being around without being a pain. If I have to force her to act like an adult, I will.

"Fine." She stands and follows me to the restroom and slams the door shut behind us. "What do you want?"

I point to the counter. "Sit." Of course, being the baby that she is, she drags her feet to sit on top of the counter. "Look, I know you don't like Justin, but that doesn't mean you have to be such a bitch to him." She opens her mouth to argue but I cut her off, "I'm not playing Tiffany. He's here, we are dating, and there's nothing you can do about it. It would make things a hell of a lot easier if you would just be nice to him for once."

"Are you seriously chastising me like I'm a child?"

"Yeah. If you're going to act like one, I'm going to treat you like one."

She sighs and shakes her head. "I can't make any promises, but I'll try. I know things seem to be going great right now, but I worry about what happens if he dumps you again."

"I'm a big girl, Tiffany. I'll be able to handle it if it comes to that."

She hops off the counter and throws her arms around me. "I hope so because you were a mess the last time it happened. I'm just trying to look out for you."

"Isn't it supposed to be the other way around," I laugh. "Don't worry about me. I can handle myself now."

"It's about time." She squeezes me to her one more time before letting go. "Well let's go hash out this bachelorette weekend party."

Spencer and Justin are sitting next to each other at the table talking quietly when we get back. Tiffany sits down on the other side of Spencer, and Justin stands to move. "Sit back down," she mumbles. He falters for a second.

"Seriously, sit down. I'm going to do my best to not be an asshole to you."

Justin eyes her warily, "This isn't some sort of trick is it?"

"No," she sighs. "No trick. I'm trying to be a grown-up."

Spencer Snickers, and Tiffany elbows him in the ribs. "What happened to being an adult?"

"Don't press your luck, Babe. You still have to go home with me."

This time I laugh, and she shoots me a glare. "Calm down, Tiff." I pull a notebook out of my bag and set it on the table in front of me. "We have a ton of planning to do."

"Why do we have to be here for this?" Spencer complains as he dips a french fry into a pile of ketchup. "We aren't the ones getting married. Besides, Johnny doesn't have us doing all kinds of stuff."

"Because I said." And that's it. That is Tiffany's entire explanation on why they have to be here. Spencer must realize he's not going to get anything else because he continues eating his fries and shuts up. I'm almost certain they will do something low-key like a bonfire, or something. That seems to be all Stella attends these days.

"I think that went pretty well," Justin guides me to the car and opens the passenger side door for me. I could drive, but I'm grateful he does it. Arguing with my cousin wears me out. She's so stubborn. He's right, though, it could have been so much worse. I was prepared for outright tantrums because she wasn't getting her way. Maybe she really is growing up.

"Yeah, I just need to call and make reservations." I

watch him round the car and get behind the steering wheel. He reaches under the seat to scoot it back. It's not a problem I have since I'm short, but his knees were touching the wheel and that had to be uncomfortable. "Thanks for coming tonight, by the way. I know it probably wasn't the highlight of your night, or what you really wanted to be doing."

He starts the car and puts it in reverse. "It's all good. I think I know why the both of y'all insisted on me and Spencer being there. You could have told me I was going to have to play referee between the two of you."

"He's used to doing it. I didn't want to scare you off." I stare out the window. "Are we going to your place or mine?" I'm honestly fine with either option, but I'm tired of being in my apartment all the time. Everything feels so cramped.

"Yours then mine?" He flips on the blinker to head back to my building. "Nothing against your bed or anything, but mine is much bigger. My feet hang off the end of yours."

"You won't see me complaining. But I'm glad we're going to my place first. I need to grab a few things."

"Like what?"

"Clothes, for one. But I need to get the rest of my wedding prep stuff. I know there is still time to plan for it, but I want to make sure Stella has everything she needs for her big day. She shouldn't have to worry about any of the small crap that can go wrong."

He pulls onto the road in front of my place. "Why doesn't Tiffany help with any of that? She sounded pretty capable at the diner."

I can't help the laugh that bursts from my lips. "Are you serious? Stella and I had to pick her last roommate.

She kept letting flaky, and even questionable, people move in, and we couldn't let her throw safety out the window anymore." He raises his eyebrows at my admission. "Seriously, I love her to death. She's one of my best friends, but she has zero organization skills. It's just not one of her strong suits. Mingling and throwing killer parties are more her scene. She'll compliment the areas that I lack. It's a win-win situation."

"You have this all figured out, don't you?"

"I wouldn't say that," I pull my hair into a side ponytail. "I just know how to use my strengths and those of others. Why make the work harder on myself in areas I know nothing about? It's why I put Tiffany in charge of the reception."

"Is there going to be a DJ at the wedding?" It's like he has no clue what happens at these events. Didn't his dad have another wedding when he married Corinne's mom?

"Yes, but even better…Tiffany talked Crooked Halo into playing, too. How awesome is that?" It really is. I knew she was going to try, but I assumed they would shoot her down. I know their schedule has got to be busy. They are rising to the top of the genre at such a quick pace, it's a wonder they still play at the hole in the wall bars my cousin frequents.

"That's the band we heard right before our first date, right?" He glances over to see my nod. "I think they'll be great. And it'll give me an excuse to get you out on the dance floor."

"Not in front of a bunch of strangers." I reach over the console and grab his hand. "Besides, I haven't even officially invited you to the wedding."

"Oh, I'm going. So, you better go ahead and add the plus on to your little RSVP list I'm sure you have." He gives my hand a quick squeeze before pulling into the parking garage. "I'll also be there for all the pre-wedding events. You aren't going to shake me so easily."

"We'll see about that." I quietly unbuckle my seat belt. As soon as he has the car in park, I open the door and take off at a sprint toward the elevator. Childish, maybe. But we used to do this all the time in high school. The only difference is back then we were surrounded by trees and now it's concrete.

I glance back to see him climbing out of the car. "There you go again," he calls out. "Always running from me. Just know that I'll never be far behind." He presses the lock button on the key fob and jogs after me. I know he can run faster than that. I mean, he did it in a suit. He likes this little game of cat and mouse, I think.

He's catching up and I press the button for the elevator over and over again. Why is this thing so damn slow? I definitely need to make a complaint to the owners about this. What if I was in actual danger?

The doors finally open and before I step on foot inside, Justin's arms are around my waist, and his mouth is next to my ear. "Told you I wouldn't be far behind."

"That's really not a fair assessment. It's not like this garage is huge." I lean into him and let him lead me into the elevator. "A toddler could have caught up to me."

"Talk about unfair. I don't think the comparison is, either." He lets go of me long enough to glance around the elevator to make sure we're alone and backs me up to the wall. "I caught you."

"You did," I smirk. "What are you going to do about it?" I still can't get over how different I feel when I'm with him. I feel empowered. Like I can ask for anything and he won't laugh.

"I can think of a few things." I don't have time to think about what he's going to do. His mouth slams onto mine and his hand dips beneath my dress.

I break away for a second. "What if someone gets on the elevator?"

"I guess I'll just have to hurry."

I don't know if it's because we could get caught or his fingers are moving at a furious pace, but I'm so close I can barely hold in my moans. He sucks on my ear lobe and slips another finger inside of me. "Fuck," I pant. That one word spurs him on. His thumb moves over my clit and right before we reach my floor, I fall apart. "I guess this means we're not going to your place tonight."

"Not a fucking chance," he groans. "The only place we're going is your bed." That's a plan I can get on board with.

Chapter Twenty-Two

Justin

WAKING up next to Audrey is how I want to spend my
forever. You'd think we'd get tired of seeing each other,
but we don't. Aside from lunch and accidental run-ins, we
rarely see each other at work. She's busy doing her job and
I'm doing mine. She probably interacts with Carter more
than she does me since he's her direct boss.

"What time is it?" A yawn escapes at the end of the
question. Her hair is splayed out on the pillow. She looks
beautiful and ethereal. I was a dumbass all those years
ago. I could have had this perfection for the last decade
and I blew it.

"I don't know. Do we have somewhere we need to be?"
I run a finger along her jaw and she nuzzles closer to me.
It's a little warm in here, but I don't want her to move.
This, right here, is where we both belong.

"Sort of." Another yawn. "I need to talk to your sister
about the wedding and see if she can take bridal pictures. I

know she said she had some jobs coming up and I want to get Stella on her calendar before it fills up."

"It's not like she's leaving any time soon," I mutter under my breath.

Audrey pulls away from me the tiniest fraction. "I know her staying with you is putting a slight constraint on us, but I like her. Who knows, maybe she's going to move here."

"She probably will. At least, after she finishes up with some clients back home. I didn't know parents get so many pictures of their kids taken. It's like every tiny milestone warrants a celebration."

"Things are a lot different than when we were growing up, that's for sure." She tries to get up, and I hold her tight. "Justin, we need to get ready." She places a soft kiss on my forehead. "It won't be so hectic once Stella and Johnny are married."

"That's what you think. Next thing you know Spencer will propose to Tiffany." Then we'll never be alone because she'll take it upon herself to make sure it is flawless.

She laughs loud and long. "I think Tiffany will propose to him before he gets the nerve to do it."

"Why do you say that?"

"Because she's the assertive one in the relationship. Once she stopped fighting her attraction to him, she was all in. Even when she screwed up, she dressed up in cosplay and went after him." That is something I can actually imagine. Tiffany has never been one to do things half-assed.

"That makes sense." I let her get out of bed and watch her walk across the room to get her robe. Her body is magnificent in the early morning light. "What else do you need to do today?"

Sliding the robe on she turns as she ties it. "The bridal shop got my dress in so I need to go try it on. Stella wants pictures to make sure it looks okay. I think she may be as controlling as I am."

That isn't a lie. She's always been the take charge cousin. She gets shit done. Audrey does, too, but at a much quieter level. She doesn't bark orders or anything like that. She does the work in the background when she doesn't have any attention on her. "Do you want me to go with you?"

"No, I think I can try on a dress by myself." My smile turns down a fraction. "Don't give me that look. You'll be fine. I need to run errands. I'll be in Asheville with Stella next weekend and I want to grab some stuff to run by her for decorations. Luckily stores have already started putting out fall products."

That sounds like a boring day. I'll definitely let her do that alone. "Yeah, I'll pass on that. Maybe I'll see if Carter wants to do something. Or hint to Corinne that she needs to get her own place."

"First," she comes back to the bad and crawls over me until she's in my lap. "We need to figure out what we're going to do for breakfast. Maybe we can pick something up on the way to your house and feed your sister for a change."

I smirk. "I know exactly what I want for breakfast and it doesn't involve food." My fingers glide up her thigh, until I reach the knot she's tied in her robe, and I slowly pull it.

"If you keep that up, we'll never leave this bed."

"That's the plan." I untie the robe completely, grab her by the waist, and flip her over until she's underneath me. "If I had my way, we'd stay here all day and night."

"But—."

"Did you give the shop a time you'd be there?" She shakes her head. "Okay, then. Problem solved. My sister, errands, it can all wait a couple more hours."

She rolls her eyes. "I guess there could be worse ways to pass the time."

"Oh, we're doing more than passing the time. We're practicing for when we can be in a bigger space." I wink and trail my hands up and down her body. Before long she'll forget about all the plans she made for the day.

Unfortunately, she didn't forget. She gave me the few hours I asked for, at least. Now, we're sitting in a drive through line. "Is your sister going to want fried chicken?"

"Why wouldn't she?"

"I don't know," Audrey shrugs. "She seems to prefer food cooked fresh at home. I guess this just seems like the complete opposite of that."

I shake my head and chuckle. "Don't let her fool you. She loves to cook from scratch, but she's never been one to turn down fried food. She'll indulge if we bring it." It's the one thing we both love. When I visit my parents, we usually grab some chicken and head down to the lake to decompress from being around them. They aren't horrible or anything, they both like to pry. It's why Corinne came to me for a place to stay instead of going to them. I get it. I would have done the same thing in her situation.

"Are you sure?"

"Yes," I sigh. "I'm sure. We just have to make sure we grab honey for the biscuits. According to her there's no other way to eat them."

"If you say so," she scrunches her nose in disgust. "The only thing I can think of that absolutely needs honey are sopapillas. Specifically, the ones at the restaurant I go to with my cousins when Stella is town."

It's finally our turn at the window and I place our order. "Can you grab my wallet out of the glove box?"

"When did you put it in there? I didn't see you do it." She pulls it out of the compartment and hands it to me.

"Last night before you made me chase you to the elevator." I flash her a devilish grin and her cheeks grow pink. When it comes to sex, she's definitely more open now than she has ever been.

"You probably shouldn't leave your wallet in the car overnight. This isn't like back home where we didn't have to worry about people breaking into our vehicles." She tucks her hair behind her ear.

"Believe me, that was the last thing on my mind. You were my number one priority." I grab my card out and pull up to the window.

Within minutes we have our food and are about to exit the parking area. "Crap. They didn't put in honey in the bag." She looks at the line of cars behind us and grimaces. "We should go back and ask for some. I don't want to disappoint your sister and have her eat less than stellar biscuits."

That's my girl…always thinking of other people. Sometimes to her own detriment. As much as we've both changed, some things still stay the same. "It'll be fine. I think I have some in the pantry." I grab her hand and pull it to my lips, kissing each knuckle. "You know you don't need her approval, right? She loves you and I don't think you could do any wrong in her eyes." What I want to say is I love you, but I don't think she's ready to hear it. Especially with what she said before we met Tiff and Spencer last night. It's hard to date at her pace when we have all this history behind us, but I'll do it because it's what she wants.

"If you don't, I can always run to the store."

A car behind us honks and I roll my eyes. These people are so impatient. It's not like they aren't going to get stuck at the next light. And that lasts a hell of a lot longer than what I'm doing. "Rinne will survive either way. Don't give it a second thought."

She shifts in her seat until she can lay her head on my shoulder. "I'll do my best, but I'm not making any promises."

"That's all I ask." I pull out of the lot before any other rude drivers start their nonsense. I really hope we get lucky and hit this light just right. If not, it's going to take us another twenty minutes to get to my house.

A car I don't recognize is parked behind my car. Maybe Corinne got a rental while her car is in the shop. That's the only possible reason. Otherwise, that would mean she has someone over and I'm not okay with that. "Who is that?" Audrey points to the car.

"I have no idea, but we're about to find out." I turn off the car and hand Audrey her keys. I don't want to misplace them before she has to leave. It'd be a good way to get her to stay, though. As much as I think I could be that devious, I can't. I know she needs to get wedding stuff done today and I don't want Stella's anger raining down on me. I've seen her pissed and I'm not a fan.

I grab the bag holding the chicken and sides from the

backseat. Audrey tries to take it out of my hand, but I don't let her. "Can you grab the drinks?"

"Sure," she nods. She opens the door then puts one of the drinks in the crook of her elbow, and grabs the drink box holding the other two. You'd think they'd upgrade to something that carries at least four drinks. "Need me to get the door for you?"

"I've got it. It's only two bags." Once she's out of the car she bumps the door closed with her hip. Normally, she'd walk right into the house. But I think after Corinne walked in on us, the thought of going inside and seeing something she can't unsee is keeping her glued to the sidewalk until I join her.

I push the door open and see Corinne pacing in the hallway. "I hope you're hungry, we brought chicken."

"Mom and your dad are here," she frantically whispers. I go to the kitchen and set the bags on the counter. What the hell? Why are they just dropping in? It's not like it's a short drive. They didn't even tell me they were planning to come this way. And whose car are they driving? That's not the same one they had the last time I visited over Christmas.

"Why didn't you warn me? I don't want to deal with them today."

"There wasn't time." She's fidgeting with her hair and I have a feeling they are here because of her.

I hear Audrey close the door behind her and I hurry to intercept her before she walks into what I'm sure will be madness in a few minutes. Not just because of whatever Corinne has to do with it, but because I've been keeping her my own little secret.

Within steps of the entryway, I hear dad's voice. Fuck, I'm too late. "Audrey, what are you doing here?"

My feet skid to a stop behind Dad and I can see the look on her face. Her eyes are as big as saucers and her mouth is wide open. She moves her lips to talk but nothing comes out. "Dad," I admonish.

"What?"

"You're being rude." I'm hoping by getting on to him, Audrey will find her words and the shock will pass by. It doesn't. She sets the drinks on the table, opens the door, and runs out of the house. "Audrey, wait."

I start for her and don't make it far. My dad grabs my arm. "We need to talk. It looks like both you and your sister have been hiding things from us."

"Last time I checked, we're both adults and don't need you butting into our lives." I yank my arm out of his hold and rush to the door. The engine turns over and by the time I make it to the driveway, she's gone. Fuck.

Chapter Twenty-Three

Audrey

I CAN'T BELIEVE I froze like that. What the hell is wrong with me? I didn't even give Justin a chance to explain. For all I know he didn't even know his dad was going to be in town. That's something he would have mentioned. At least, I hope he would.

I pull over at a gas station down the road from Justin's house and grab my phone out of my bag. I tap the last number I dialed. The phone rings three times before she picks up. "Tiffany, are you home? I need to come over."

"Slow down, what's going on?" She sounds out of breath and I don't want to know what she was doing. At least she answered.

"I'll tell you when I get there."

"Audrey, right now isn't exactly a good time," she sighs. I hear her hand cover the receiver and she mumbles something to someone I can only assume is Spencer. "Okay, come over. How far out are you?"

"Maybe fifteen minutes."

"Okay, I'll be ready." She hangs up before I can say anything else.

Tears blur my eyes. I don't even know why I'm crying. It's not like his dad even said anything mean to me. At least to anyone looking it wouldn't be. I've just spent so much of my life wondering why that man hated me so much. Him asking why I was there sounded accusatory, and as if I didn't belong.

My phone starts dinging with messages and I turn it off before getting back on the road. It's a good thing I'm not going home. That would be the first place he checks. He also doesn't have Tiffany's number so he can't call her. Right now, I need to be away. I need to wrap my head around how things are going to work with Justin when his dad obviously doesn't want me around.

Twenty minutes later thanks to the stupid red light I hate, I'm standing in front of Tiffany's door. I knock three times and Spencer answers the door. "She's in the living room."

"Thanks," I mutter. I'm probably overreacting. I hope I am. Even though I haven't said it yet, I love Justin. I always have and I always will. I've only been asking him to take things slow just in case he breaks my heart again. I didn't want to get too close and then have it all ripped away…again.

The door closes behind me as I make my way to the sofa. It looks so different in here with Spencer's touch. There are comic posters on the side of the wall and he's added his DVD collection to the shelf under the TV. It's mundane and perfect. They balance each other out and have small pieces of both of them peppered through the apartment.

"You're here. What took so long?" Tiffany pats the space beside her. "I took the precaution and poured you a glass of wine."

"Red light." I take the glass of wine she offers me and down it in one go. It's a decent wine and I wonder if it's from the winery by Stella. It definitely tastes like it.

"Wow. She downed that thing like a shot." It's only then that I notice the computer sitting on the coffee table and Stella's face filling the screen. Her eyebrows are furrowed and she looks concerned.

"You called her? She has other stuff to do, she doesn't need to worry about me."

Tiffany shrugs. "It sounded like boy problems and you know we only ever hash that out together." She doesn't add the I told you so even though I know she wants to.

Spencer grabs my glass and goes to refill it. Stella on the other hand has her eyes on me. "What happened?"

I tell them about Justin's dad being there when we walked in, and they gasp. They know my history with him and aren't as surprised as I am about my own reaction. "I just ran. It's apparently the only thing I know how to do when I'm confronted with my past."

"Did he sound mad?" Tiffany asks. She motions for Spencer to get her a glass of wine and I hand her mine. I don't want it. I just needed something in the moment.

"I couldn't really tell. I sort of freaked out." I pause replaying the scene in my mind. "But he said something about Justin and Corinne keeping secrets from him."

"He never told his dad y'all were back together?" Tiffany shrieks. "That's absolutely insane. It's been a couple of months."

That's what has me second guessing everything. "In Justin's defense, he doesn't really talk to his dad much anymore. He visits for holidays and that's pretty much it."

"Don't defend him," Tiffany scoffs.

"Tiff," Stella admonishes her. "Chill. Audrey, why did you run?"

"Because I spent most of high school trying to get that man to like me. Wanting him to approve of my relationship with Justin." I take a deep breath. This is where I lay all of my insecurities out on the line for my cousins. "Both of you know why Justin broke up with me then and I thought today would end up as a replay of that night. I love him and I don't see how a relationship between us is going to prosper if his dad sticks his nose in our business and is dead set against it."

"So, basically you want his dad's approval?" Stella asks.

Do I? I take a few moments to let that sink in. I guess so. Or, at least a reason why he doesn't like me. Anything at this point. "That seems to be the root of the issue. I've loved Justin since I was sixteen and I never stopped. I don't even know if Justin said anything to him after I left, or if he tried to come after me."

Stella sighs over the screen. "He did. He's been blowing up Johnny's phone wondering if we've heard from you."

"What did you tell him?"

"That you're fine and you'll go over there when you're ready." I can hear her tapping her finger against her laptop. "Do you think you'll ever be okay with his dad not liking, or approving, your dating?"

"I honestly don't know." I pull a strand of my hair in front me and start braiding the ends. "I'd like to say yes, but I'm not sure I can handle any animosity from his dad if we are around him."

Tiffany turns until she's facing me completely. "I can't believe I'm saying this," she mutters. "If you love him as much as you say you do and he feels the same way, you're going to have to confront his dad. Stand your ground and let him know the two of you aren't going to let him push you around."

"I'm not good at that. I just want him to like me. To think I'm good enough for his son."

"No," Tiffany butts in. "That's not what matters. Your only focus should be Justin regardless of what his dad says or feels. You'll just have to get used to not being liked by everyone. Look at me, I don't give a rat's ass what people think of me. As long as I'm happy, they can live in their own little world."

She has a point, and as much as I don't want to admit it…she's giving me solid advice. "When did you become so wise?"

"I have two pretty amazing cousins who taught me everything I know." She pulls me into her arms. "So, are you doing this thing? Or, are you going to give up again and let his dad dictate what happens between the two of you?"

"No," I yell, a little too loud. "My happiness will not be held in the palm of his dad's hand. I'm going to stand up for myself."

"That's my girl," Stella claps. "Tiff, go with her in case she freaks again and needs an escape. Spencer, stay on standby."

"Why?" He scratches his head in confusion.

"Because if everything goes the way we want it, you'll need to pick up Tiffany." She claps her hands together like she's coaching a team. "Now, get a move on. First, Audrey, you need to go get cleaned up. You look like a mess."

"Gee, thanks," I mumble. Without any more prompting I get up and head to Tiffany's room. She'll have whatever I need in there. I can do this. Be strong and fight for what you want.

"Do you need me to go up to the door with you?" Tiffany asks from the passenger seat. We're parked on the street across from Justin's driveway. His dad is still there and I can feel my throat closing up.

I won't let his dad scare me into not being with the person I love. "No." I put the car in drive and park next to what I can only assume is the car his dad and step-mom drove in with. Turning the car off I get out of the car. "Here's the keys just in case."

"Go get your man. You've got this." Tiff throws her fist in the air, cheering me on.

My steps are slow and steady as I make my way to the door. The curtains are closed and nobody can see me approach. I take three deep breaths and raise my hand. There are raised voices coming from the house, but I don't care. I have to do this. Not only for me, but for Justin. He needs to know I'm strong enough to stand up for myself. I ignore the doubt bubbling up in my stomach and knock.

Chapter Twenty-Four

Justin

DAMN IT. She ran without even looking back to see if I'd follow. I know she is leery about my dad since he wasn't exactly the kindest person to her, but I didn't realize it went so deep. I pull out my phone and try to call her. It rings once then goes to voicemail. I press her number again and it goes straight to voicemail. She turned her phone off. I hope she realizes I didn't purposefully spring this on her. I had no clue my dad was going to surprise us with a visit today. He usually gives me a heads up, at least.

Rushing back into the house, I find Corinne staring at the window. She can't see anything outside because the curtains are still covering them. "Where are the keys to my car?"

That pulls her attention away from wherever her thoughts took her. "They're on the key hook I installed last week. I'll go get them."

"You can't go running off, Son. I didn't come here for my own—." My dad starts to say, but I glare at him

"You don't get to tell me what to do in my own house." I grab the keys off the hook and throw the door open. "Stay, or go, I don't really care. Just know that if you stay you will treat me *and* Audrey with respect. Corinne, are you coming or staying?"

She doesn't have to be asked twice. She grabs her wallet off the table and hightails it out of the house in front of me. Once we're tucked into my car, she finally speaks up. "I would have warned you if I had time. They were jumping my ass right before you pulled in."

That's news to me. "Why would they be mad at you?" I mean, sure, she's been here longer than I was prepared for, but she's an adult and can do whatever she wants.

"Because my ex has been out of my place for a month?" Her voice pitches higher at the end. Scared I'm going to bitch her out. That's not my style. It would have been nice if she was upfront with me, but I get it. After years of growing up with a father that questions your every fucking move, I do my best to not pry.

"Okay, but that can't be all there is." I pull out of the driveway and head toward downtown. Toward Audrey.

"I may have also put my house and studio on the market." Ah, so that's what they are pissed about. She's fleeing the nest and they worry they won't be able to dictate what she does. Not that they've done it to the extent Dad has me, but still.

"So, that's why you've been here so long." I don't phrase it as a question. It's not. "You know you could have told me, right? I wouldn't have run off to them to tattle."

"I know that." She rolls down the window a bit to get some fresh air. All it does is let the heat roll into the car. "I wanted to do it on my own, though. I *should* be able to, anyway. It's a lot harder to find what I'm looking for in this area. I need a space big enough for me, but also to have an in-house studio. I don't want to rent a ridiculously over-priced space I barely use."

Audrey was right. My sister fell in love with the city. "We'll get you set up. Assuming I can get Audrey to talk to me again, maybe you can take over the lease in her apartment until you find something. You still have jobs lined up, right?"

"Yeah. I've been updating my website and have quite a few inquiries. At this rate, I'm actually going to have to use my calendar." She shudders. She's always been able to keep up with the small-town people wanting photos. The way of life is slower-paced. But here? It's another world. And there are so many more potential clients. I'm honestly shocked she didn't try to make the move sooner.

"That's good. First up, we find Audrey. After that, we'll have a talk with our parents." It's past time they started living their own lives and stopped worrying about what we're doing with ours.

Less than thirty minutes later I'm in front of Audrey's door. I didn't see her car in her usual spot, and she's probably not here, but I need to make sure. My knuckles tap the door harder than I expect and I jump at the loudness of it. "Audrey," I call out in case she's in her bedroom. No answer. I go through this three more times and admit defeat.

On the way back to my car, I pull out my phone to see if Stella's fiancé has texted me back. I just want to know that she's good. That is what's most important more than anything else. I open the car door and sigh as I slide behind the steering wheel. "No luck?" Corinne is peeking around me, hoping to see my girl following.

"Nope," I grunt. "My guess is she's at Tiffany's but I

don't have her number or address." There's not much left to do other than go home and wait for Audrey to get in touch. "Will you keep an eye on my phone?"

"Sure," she grabs it out of my hand. "Why?"

"I'm waiting on a message from her soon-to-be cousin-in-law." Fingers crossed he has enough empathy for me to respond. I don't see why he wouldn't, especially since he texted me that first night I ran into Audrey to let me know she was okay.

Corinne is scanning through the radio stations as I drive and while normally that would annoy me, it's keeping my mind off the thought of losing Audrey once again because of my old man. We're almost home when my phone beeps with a message. "Who is it?"

Corinne holds the phone to my face to unlock it. "It's an unknown number, but it says she's fine. Just give her a bit."

"Thank God." I breathe a sigh of relief. At least I know she's okay. Now, I need to take care of the next mess. How does one prepare to tell your dad to accept who you love or shove it?

Well, they didn't leave. I nudge Corinne with my elbow. "Are you ready for this?"

"Not even a little bit," she shakes her head. "But it has to be done. At some point, they have to let go. We aren't their puppets to control."

"I think my dad has been controlling me much longer than your mom has you." I open the door and get out of the car.

"Let's not turn this into who has the crappiest

parent." She gets out and comes to stand beside me. "They are both awesome and suck to a certain extent. We just have to roll with the bunches and hope they understand."

Walking into the house, it looks like they haven't moved the entire time we've been gone. I fully expected them to make themselves at home. I guess me blowing up at Dad freaked them out a bit. I've never done that before. Not even when I was a teenager. I would halfway listen then go to my room to blow off steam. I don't have the energy to do that anymore.

"You're finally back," Dad stands up from the couch. "It sounds like we all need to have a talk."

"If you are going to spend this time to bitch us out for the choices we make, then you can leave. This is my home and we're adults. As long as you're here, you'll respect that." I feel like Stella and Tiffany would be proud of me for standing up to him. Maybe, even Audrey would be, too.

"How long have you and Audrey been dating, and where did you reconnect?" He crosses his arms over his chest in an act of intimidation. Sadly, that doesn't work with me anymore. I've been taller than him for years.

"Not that it's any of your business," I begin. He may want to prove that he's the bigger man, but I don't care. The only thing that will piss him off more is if I show that *he* doesn't bother me. I sit down on the chair closest to the couch. "We ran into each other when the company merged. I found out she was an employee of the other company."

"Jesus, Son." Dad runs a hand down his face. "Are you out of your mind? First you stick to her like glue as a teenager, then you work with her and you decide it's a good time to date? Do you have any idea what that could do to your career?"

"Oh, did I mention I'm one of her bosses?" That will be the icing on the freaking cake.

"Are you serious?" He roars. "You are making a huge mistake once again. I don't know what it is about that girl that makes you lose all common sense, but it needs to end. What is it this time? Some kind of office fetish between the two of you? When your bosses find out…" He's standing over me and that was the last line I'll allow him to cross.

I get up from the chair and he has to take a step back. "They will do nothing." My teeth are clenched and I'm barely holding in my rage. "There's nothing against it in the handbook. I checked. And that's the last time you will *ever* say anything bad about the woman I love. If you can't find it in your heart to accept her, then you can stop talking to me. End of discussion. I won't continue to allow you to make her feel like shit."

Just then I hear a voice in the entryway. "You love me?" My mouth drops open at the sight of her.

Corinne rolls her eyes. "I tried to get your attention, but you were too busy telling your dad off. Bravo, by the way."

"Corinne," her mother spits.

"Nope, you and I can have this conversation outside," she points at her mom. "If you'll follow me." I'm happy she's standing up for herself, too. They never really approved of her career choice but didn't say much about it because she takes care of herself. The two of them leave without a backward glance.

"That wasn't exactly how I wanted to tell you," I shrug. "But yes, I do."

"I love you, too." She launches herself at me. Arms

around my neck, clinging to me like I'm the most important thing in her life. She's right where she belongs and I feel a sense of relief that we might just be okay.

"Give me a break," Dad mutters. And the relief is gone.

"Look, Mr. Petersen, I don't know what I did to make you hate me, but I'm done letting you make me feel like crap. I've done nothing but love your son since we were sixteen. I never stopped." She stands tall next to me and I beam with pride. There's that fire she's always kept hidden. "You'll either respect me, or you won't. That's your choice, but I don't have to allow it."

"I can't believe how ridiculous you two are. Nothing has changed. It's like watching you in high school all over again," he grunts.

"Well, until you can accept it, you can leave." I lead Audrey to the kitchen. "Stay right here, I'll be back." She nods and I go back to the living room. "I wasn't playing, Dad. If you can't act like the adult you claim you are, go home. When you're done with whatever it is that's made you dislike her from such a young age, then you can call me. Until then...don't bother."

Dad's mouth opens wide and he stomps past me. He doesn't say another word. I watch him walk out the door, pausing long enough to tell his wife to come on, and they get in the car. Just like that he's gone.

I don't know Audrey is right behind me until she wraps her arms around my waist. "I'm sorry."

I turn until my eyes meet hers. "Don't be. That man has more hate in his heart than anyone I've ever met. You will always be worth it."

"I didn't want to cause a rift between the two of you." She pulls me tighter. "He's the reason I ran earlier. Not you, never you again. I'm back where I was always meant to be."

"Audrey, you're my home." I bend down until my lips touch and I could get lost in them for hours. Corinne clears her throat behind me. "First, we have to find her a place to live. I'm certain both of us have been disowned."

"I'm betting probably so," Audrey laughs. "We'll find you a place."

"Thanks, sis." Corinne rushes and throws her arms around the both of us. "Welcome to the family...again."

Yeah, she definitely needs her own place. She's cramping my style. How am I supposed to knock Audrey's socks off if my sister is here?

Epilogue

Audrey

"I THOUGHT you said Johnny was easy going?" We're at our favorite Mexican restaurant, going over last-minute wedding preparations. "He has Spencer running around trying to find these obscure snacks his brother likes."

All I can do is laugh. The only time I've ever seen him this keyed up is when he was getting ready to pop the question at the ski resort. "He has a weird relationship with his sibling. Just go with it."

"If you say so." He takes a chip from the middle of the table and dips it into the salsa. "I can promise you I won't be like that when we get married."

I turn my head in his direction so fast, I could be that little girl in The Exorcist. "Excuse me?" This better not be the way he decided to ask me to marry him. I just might murder him.

"When, and if, we decide to get married, I'm leaving all of this to you." He sees the look on my face and backtracks. "I mean, I'll do whatever you tell me to do." That's better.

"You say that, now," I grin. I steal the chip he's about to put in his mouth. "Will you be upset if your dad is still not on speaking terms with you when that day comes?"

He stares at me, the chip, and his now empty hand. Seriously, that's what he thinks is the most important part? He grabs another chip with the hand furthest from me. "Honestly, I don't know. But if he's going to be disrespectful, I don't want him there anyway. He'd do his best to make the day miserable for us." He grabs my hand and kisses my open palm. "That's not what I want when it's our turn. It will be special, magical, and everything you deserve."

And I think my panties melted off of their own accord. Back then he put me above all else as much as he could under his dad's roof, and we had to deal with it. Now, though, we can make our own rules and write our own story. "I love you."

He opens his mouth, but Tiffany yells across the table. "If y'all don't start paying attention, I'm going to split you up."

Justin pulls me so close, I'm almost in his lap. "You can try."

"Do you really want to go that route?" She lifts an eyebrow.

"On second thought," Justin clears his throat. "What were you saying?"

I don't miss Spencer laughing at the way he backs down to my baby cousin. He's known her most of her life, though. He knows *exactly* how ruthless Tiffany can be.

I snuggle further into him, and relish the feel of his

arms around me. I thought running into him after a
decade would be the worst thing that could happen to me.
Turns out, I found love again.

Welcome to Your Life Prologue

There's nothing like sitting around a bonfire in the beginning of summer. It's already hot as Hades, and this whole shindig is ridiculous. I know it's supposed to be our last big party since we graduated a few hours ago, but I'm pretty much over it. It's the same people and the same place. Doesn't anyone get tired of seeing each other all the damn time?

I'm in shorts and a tank top, standing as far away from the monstrosity of flames as I can, and I'm still sweating. I'm surprised the police haven't been called out here by concerned neighbors. The flames are definitely high enough to be seen from town. But I guess being in the middle of a field on private property keeps that from happening. Jake and his buddies didn't plan this well at all. We should be at a pool somewhere, or hell, even the lake. Everyone thought it was a great idea since the star athlete suggested it. I voiced my opinion, but it went unheard.

Jake is standing with a few of his friends as I head

toward him. I don't feel like being here anymore. I'd much rather be home, curled up in bed and reading a book.

"I'm ready to go," I tell Jake when I reach him. He completely ignores me, like he always does when we're at these parties. Don't get me wrong, he's a nice guy, but when he starts drinking he goes into asshole mode.

I tap him on the arm, "I said I'm ready to go, Jake."

He whirls around on me. And I can already tell by that glazed look in his eyes that he's going to be a jerk.

"Well, I'm not. Go hang out with Cami, or something." He glares at me, daring me to argue with him.

"Cami is hooking up with some guy. It's hot, and I'm tired of standing around." I know I should keep my mouth closed, but I don't like being told what to do.

"Too damn bad, Tonya. I'm not leaving, so chill the fuck out." He roars, making sure his point is made.

This statement right here pisses me off more than anything. I don't understand why he thinks he can treat me like shit when he starts drinking. Is it some kind of man code or something? I know some of the other guys don't act like this, but the sad fact is, most of them do.

I stare Jake down, and when he won't give an inch, I unleash. "Who the hell do you think you are? We've been dating a long time, but that does not mean you can talk to me like I'm worthless." I take a deep breath before continuing, "I'm leaving, and I don't care if I have to *walk* all the way home." I shout. "I'm tired of this shit, and can't take it anymore."

I notice everything has gone eerily quiet, and I glance around. Just fucking great. We've attracted a crowd. That was not my intention, but I can't deal with this anymore. It's the same thing every weekend, and I'm just tired of it. I love Jake, or at least, I want to. It would be so much easier that way. He's the golden boy of our high school and everyone keeps telling me I should be grateful that he picked me. And I was for a long time. But now – now everything just feels strained. Disconnected. We've started drifting apart and most days I feel like I'm just going through the motions. Like we both are. Staying together because it's easier than breaking up. Definitely easier than being alone. Or at least it was, but I'm over being treated like his pretty little lapdog.

I start walking toward the driveway, and come to a halt when I hear him yelling behind me.

"That's okay bitch, keep walking. Now I don't have to deal with your moody ass anymore." He's laughing like he doesn't have a care in the world.

I want to beat the hell out of him so bad. But I don't really want to cause any more of a scene. I already know that I'll be the talk of the town tomorrow, and giving them more fuel to gossip wouldn't be a good idea. I flip Jake the finger and continue on my merry way.

I should probably call my parents to come pick me up, but I'm a little buzzed and don't want to get a lecture. Their little vacation to celebrate my graduation means they aren't home anyway. Walking is probably the dumbest idea I've had today. Well… besides telling Jake off in front of everyone. That ranks right up there at the top.

I come to stop when I know I'm far enough away from the party that nobody will see me, and pull out my phone to call Cami. I'm sure she's already heard about what happened, but I need her just the same. The ringing from the phone sounds loud compared to the still quiet of the night.

Finally, she picks up. "Oh my gosh, what happened? Where are you? Dammit T, answer me."

Even though I'm beyond frustrated I can't help but chuckle. Only she would get worked up into a tizzy without letting me explain anything.

"I'm fine. I'm down the road. Any chance you want to pick me up, and take me home?" I ask.

"Not a problem at all. I'll be there in just a sec."

"Thanks," I breathe, right before hanging up.

Cami is on her way, but I still keep walking. I want to put as much distance between Jake and myself as I can. But just thinking about that asshat has me fuming once again.

Before I can march back to the party and give him a piece of my mind, a car pulls up beside me.

The window comes down, and Cami leans toward it. "Get in, hot stuff."

I smile and slide into the car. Cami looks at me expectantly. I know she wants all the details of what just went down, but I'm not sure if I'm ready to talk about it. I'm still angry and hurt. Finally, she lets off the brake and we make our way down the dusty, dirt road.

As we're pulling up to my driveway, I shift my body and face Cami. She puts the car in park, and stays put. Waiting for me to speak.

"I'm pretty sure I just broke up with Jake." My voice catches, and a tear slides down my face. I hate that I cry when I'm angry. It's one of my many misgivings that really pisses me off.

"Yeah, I heard," Cami replies. "But how he behaved? That was inexcusable. I didn't catch the part where you went off on him, but I heard the backlash when I was looking for my car to come pick you up."

"Oh great. I can't even imagine what he's telling everyone." I bury my face in my hands, and try to rub this horrible night out of existence.

"Don't even worry about it, girl. You did yourself a favor. Now, stop angry crying. Let's go inside and eat all the chocolate your mom has stashed in the freezer." She lifts my chin until I'm looking at her. She knows I can't resist chocolate.

"That," my voice cracks and I clear my throat. "That sounds like a fantastic idea."

This is definitely a much better way to spend graduation night. With my best friend by my side, and chocolate to eat to ease my troubles.

Acknowledgments

Whew. Writing this book was something else entirely. We went through snowpocalypse in Texas and it feels like there was just one thing after another.

I couldn't have written this book without my amazing Alpha readers. Getting messages about the story made my days so much better.

Also, my crew. Stephanie, Tasha, Ashley, & Kelsie… y'all keep me motivated. Thank you for listening to my whining and making sure I got my stuff done. But also for reminding me that sometimes it's okay to just binge watch TV for a night.

And as usual, my family, without your unwavering support I wouldn't be able to fall into my stories and bring the characters to life.

And readers, without you, the stories would be sitting in files on my computer. Thank you for taking a chance on me and diving into my books.

Also by Katrina Marie

Cousins Gone RomCom Series

Gone Country

Gone Steady

Gone Inn

Gone Before

Gone Again

Out of the Ashes Series

The Taking Chances Series

Cocky Hero Club

Big Baller

Baseball & Broadway

About the Author

Katrina Marie lives in the Dallas area with her husband, two children, and fur baby. She is a lover of all things geeky. When she's not writing you can find her at her children's sporting events, or curled up reading a book.
Visit her online: katrinamarieauthor.com
Sign up for her newsletter http://
bit.ly/KatrinaMarieNewsletter